double

Georges Simenon

The Delivery

Translated from the French by
Eileen Ellenbogen

A Helen and Kurt Wolff Book
Harcourt Brace Jovanovich
New York and London

Library of Congress Cataloging in Publication Data

Simenon, Georges, 1903–
The delivery.

Translation of Bergelon.
"A Helen and Kurt Wolff book."
I. Title.
PQ2637.I53B413   1981   843'.912   80–8759
ISBN 0–15–124655–6

Printed in the United States of America

First American edition 1981

B C D E

The Delivery

Chapter One

One did not have to be a doctor to diagnose Bergelon's trouble: he was suffering from a hangover. It was
not an altogether unpleasant sensation, at least not as
long as he stayed in bed. He was sweating, and he had
the feeling that all his weariness, everything inside him
that was bad, was slowly oozing out through his skin.
Moreover, he was itching, as though he had a healing
scar.

Later it would be different. When he got out of bed he
would have a headache. He would feel dizzy. For the
present he merely felt lightheaded, with bittersweet
thoughts passing through his mind. He did not find this
disagreeable; it was no bad thing to indulge in a brief fit
of melancholy from time to time.

Mechanically, he touched the place beside him in the

bed, thus discovering, without opening his eyes, that Germaine was already up. This was the inescapable cloud on the horizon. She would not utter a word of reproach, but she would be sad all day and, worse, gentle in her sadness. As for himself, he knew beforehand that he would not be able to avoid mumbling:

"I think I must have had a drop too much to drink last night."

His wife would respond, with a gesture of resignation:
"Think nothing of it."

But this would not prevent Bergelon from hovering at her side, making excuses for himself, attempting to prove that it had not been his fault, that, if anything, it had been all to the good. . . .

With his eyes still closed, he frowned. A fly had landed on his nose. The window was open. The room was bathed in sunlight, and the street outside was deserted. The feel of the day was so familiar to him: no grocer's van with its tooting horn; no slamming of doors as the occupants of the houses, mostly humble employees, set out for work.

And besides, church bells were ringing for Mass. It was Sunday. Germaine was taking off her coat in the hall. She was just back from Saint-Nicolas, where she had attended the seven o'clock Communion service.

Doors could be heard to slam, and there was the sound of hobnail boots on wood, chipping bits out of the pine treads of the stairs. No doubt about it, Emile was off to a Boy Scout meeting, while his sister would be hogging the bathroom for the next hour.

Emile must have been sorely tempted to wake his father, to ask for the extra money that, without his mother's knowledge, Bergelon usually gave him on Sundays.

The table was being laid. Water was boiling on the gas ring—they never lit the kitchen range on Sundays.

Then, all of a sudden, Bergelon felt a kind of inward jolt. It was this almost imperceptible sensation that began it all. It was exactly like the start of an illness.

"Have you had any pain or discomfort recently?" he would ask his patients.

"I think so. Every now and then, especially when I wake up in the morning, a sort of dull ache in my chest."

"How long has this been going on?"

For him these were routine questions, part of the daily round. For them those few minutes spent in his consulting room, after they had sat on the little chairs upholstered in green velvet in the waiting room, represented a decisive turning point. Symptoms that until then had been nothing more than barely noticeable twinges were identified by name, and suddenly the patient was someone suffering from an illness.

He was now sweating even more profusely. He was on the point of opening his eyes and endeavoring to clear his mind, when he thought better of it and decided to doze on for a few more minutes.

A face . . . the kind of immature, boyish face with something sharp about it nevertheless, wearing an expression that was both anxious and aggressive; he had seen so many in his office, and they nearly all asked the same question:

"Is it *that*?"

He could feel them trembling. He could see the little beads of moisture covering the space between nose and upper lip.

But this had been different. Cosson, the son of the former local policeman—he had been Bergelon's patient and had died of cancer of the stomach—had looked at him with an air of more intense suffering, perhaps even of menace.

He turned over in bed. It really was time he got up. The door opened. It was Emile.

"Are you awake?"

He opened his eyes, and there was his son, long legged and knob-kneed, in his Boy Scout uniform.

"There's some money in the pocket of my trousers. You can have ten francs."

It was another unpleasant shock to see Emile holding up the trousers that matched Bergelon's dinner jacket. For he scarcely ever wore his dinner jacket, not even once a year The dinner jacket reminded him of the surgeon, Mandalin. Mandalin reminded him of the clinic in the Ville-Haute, and the gardens full of tulips, and Jean Cosson pacing up and down with long, restless strides.

"Is your mother back?"

He knew she was, but he asked just the same. The unfamiliar taste in his mouth was the aftertaste of whisky, which he had drunk at Mandalin's while they were playing bridge. He must have looked like a fool. They had asked him if he played contract bridge, and he had replied that of course he did. He had been carried away, as he always was when he drank. He had overbid his hand repeatedly; then, to make matters worse, he had argued stubbornly in defense of his errors.

"Where are you going today?"

"To the woods at Méran. The Wolf Cubs are blazing three trails and . . ."

The ringing of a bell downstairs in the office. The telephone. Germaine's voice answering it and then calling upstairs:

"Elie, it's for you."

He grabbed his purple dressing gown and put it on as he went downstairs. He now had a very severe headache. He caught a glimpse of his wife and daughter in the dining room.

"Hello, Doctor Bergelon speaking."

He recognized the voice at once:

"Is that you, old man?"

Mandalin had the habit of addressing everyone as "old man."

"How is it going? . . . Not too much of a thick head, I hope? . . . Look, I'm calling you about the Cosson woman. My wife and I have a luncheon engagement in La Sologne. We'll be leaving in a few minutes. . . . It might be a good thing, don't you think, if you looked in at the clinic? . . ."

Bergelon's hands were shaking, but probably only because he had had too much to drink the night before.

"Any new developments?" he asked.

"I've just had a call from the nurse on the case. . . . There's been no change. . . ."

"Well?"

"Nothing . . . What do you expect me to do about it, old man? . . . I'll be back this evening. . . . I'll call you then. Give my regards to your wife."

And that was that! He stood there motionless, then slowly replaced the receiver.

Why should he be the one to go to the clinic? Was he the surgeon? Had he attended Cosson's wife's delivery at three o'clock in the morning?

He was miles away when his son, standing on tiptoe, kissed him on the forehead and rushed out into the street, slamming the door so violently that the whole house shook.

"One of these days he'll break it."

Germaine could always be trusted to fear the worst and to prophesy doom with quiet resignation.

"Don't you want your breakfast?"

There was no escaping her first uneasy glance, then Annie's puzzled look. The child was dressed for church.

She was thirteen, and in all respects—in her attitudes, in her facial expressions—she was a miniature version of her mother.

No matter. As usual, he kissed them, one after the other, on both cheeks, and took his seat facing the open French windows and the little garden beyond. At the bottom of the garden, fenced in with wire mesh, was a chicken run with six cackling hens and a cockerel. An airplane, from one of the flying clubs at Bourges or Moulins, droned high up in the sky. Once again church bells were ringing, but this time from some more distant parish.

The table was covered with a blue-and-white checked cloth. Bergelon had a coffee pot all to himself, as he disliked coffee flavored with chicory and did not take milk.

Was it really such a tragic business, after all? He had a mental picture of Cosson on the grounds of the clinic as the first light of dawn glimmered in the sky. The clinic was a lovely place, set on a hill and surrounded by trees and newly built villas. Mandalin was well aware of the attractions of luxurious surroundings, and he also knew that his patients were prepared to pay much higher fees for the privilege of being nursed through their operations by pretty women who wore stylish uniforms.

To pass the time, Bergelon had gone out to smoke a cigarette. He had not been completely drunk. Indeed, he had sobered up considerably already, or so he fancied. The faintly moldy smell of damp soil rose from the earth. All the neighboring houses were still shuttered. A chauffeur, a very early riser, was hosing down a sumptuous automobile. The Loire flowed past in the valley below.

And Cosson, while his wife was in labor, was outside, bending down to look at a flower bed full of tulips.

He was feverish. It was his nature to be always in a

state of tension. As Bergelon came up to him, Cosson felt impelled to say, pointing to the flowers:

"It's an extraordinary thing, isn't it, that these flowers just come into being quite simply and painlessly, whereas ..."

He sniffed, nostrils pinched, and looked up at one of the windows of the clinic, where light glowed behind a drawn shade.

Was his distress genuine? Had it been genuine a month ago, when he had brought his wife, the daughter of a retired railroad official, to consult Bergelon about her pregnancy?

"Are you quite sure, doctor, that the child is lying as it should?"

Tense, even at that stage! Much too tense, and exhausting to be with.

Besides, he was—how could one put it?—too earnest, too sensitive, too responsive.

"Look, doctor, I'm not a rich man. I was born in this parish, and you've known me all my life. My father was a policeman. He died young, and my mother worked hard to give me a decent education. I became a cashier at the bank. I married Marthe. We own our own apartment and have all the furniture we need. It's not very fancy, but it's comfortable. What small savings I have left I wish to spend on her confinement. She must have everything she needs, including the services of the best available specialist. And if I find I can't pay all the fees at once, I will pay in monthly installments. You need only make inquiries at the bank...."

The cockerel was strutting about in the chicken run at the bottom of the garden, which was half in sunlight, half in shadow. Germaine hesitated, glancing at her daughter, groping for an appropriate euphemism, then said with a sigh:

"Did everything go well?"

Serves her right! After all, she was the one to blame. If she hadn't been forever nagging him about money . . . and always sounding on the verge of tears.

When had her parents ever had any money? What had her father ever been but a salesman of heating stoves, who personally installed the appliances he sold?

Which had not prevented her, as soon as they were married, from counting every penny they spent or from hoarding little piles of petty cash.

"It's for the gas. . . ."

Or the electricity, or the coal . . . A month in advance! The notion had never even crossed her mind that, in a pinch, the gas company could wait.

And had she not worked out to the nearest cent the cost of every single egg laid by her hens?

"Has it never occurred to you that people take advantage of you and that you could easily charge more for your visits?"

Money for money's sake, for the security it provided. She had never wanted a live-in housekeeper. The most she would agree to was a cleaning woman twice a week to do the rough work. From morning till night she was on the run, washing and ironing, dusting and mending. And if ever, by some mischance, Emile sat on the floor, she would invariably admonish him:

"You'll wear out your shorts!"

At the same time she felt deprived because the house was only two stories high. Not that they had any need for more rooms, but a three-story house was a symbol of affluence.

"Well, since you ask, no! Everything did not go all right. Far from it—it all went wrong, very wrong!"

Then he blurted it out:

"The child is dead!"

Nonetheless, that fact did not at that moment prevent him from relishing his croissant, as he watched the Leghorn cockerel flapping its wings in pursuit of a hen.

"Poor woman! She must be brokenhearted."

"She hasn't been told yet."

"Didn't she ask to see her baby?"

He looked at his daughter. He could not very well say more while she was present. Annie, sensing this, said sulkily:

"All right, I'm going. Where have you put the missal, Mother?"

For in addition to their ordinary prayer books, they owned a gilt-edged missal bound in tan morocco leather, which was used by all the family. Annie put on her white gloves. More kisses all around. In this house there was kissing all day long, whenever anyone went out or came in. It was more or less a reflex action, an absent-minded pursing of the lips, a peck without even an exchange of glances.

Now that Annie was out of the way, Bergelon could speak more openly:

"She's in a very bad way. Her chances of pulling through are slim...."

"And that poor boy?"

The poor boy would be left a widower. So what? Bergelon was sorely tempted to say as much to his wife, without mincing words.

It was all her fault, however unlikely that might seem. Take that notion of hers, about adding another story to the house. And for no better reason than that two of their neighbors had built an upper floor on their houses!

Quite by chance, one day a couple of months earlier, Bergelon had bumped into Doctor Mandalin in the street. He knew him only by sight, having seen him from time to time at Medical Association meetings. Mandalin was a respected public figure. He lived in a magnificent period house in the most affluent district of Bugle. He had built his own sumptuously equipped clinic, with accommodations for twelve patients. It was not long before he was able to employ his own chauffeur.

"I say, Bergelon, old man . . ."

As if they had been schoolmates or members of the same regiment.

"Don't for one moment imagine that I'm complaining, but you don't seem to refer many of your patients to me. . . ."

"Well, you know . . . most of my patients come from that one district. . . ."

He might have added:

"And a pretty poor district, at that."

For it was still possible to earn a living from the poor. Not, however, from his neighbors in the parish at Saint-Nicolas, who were neither rich nor poor, but who devoted all their modest resources to keeping up appearances.

"My charges are not as high as people say. I don't charge more than the patients can afford. As for yourself, you won't regret it. The entire fee for the first operation I perform on a patient of yours will be turned over to you. Thereafter you will receive half the fee for each patient. So long, old man, see you soon."

The alternative was to carry on as before, charging twenty francs a visit and continuing to endure Germaine's small-minded penny pinching.

Courting disaster seemed to be a universal human failing. . . . Take Cosson and his wife: Cosson swaggering and snuffling, swearing on what he held "dearest in all the world," that only "the best gynecologist in Bugle" was worthy to preside over the birth of his child.

Mandalin, by God! Mandalin, who was prepared to

moderate his fee; Mandalin, who there and then produced an engraved card inviting the Bergelons to dinner and bridge.

"Evening dress."

Germaine, in a panic, rushing off to the dressmaker. The pungent smell of benzine permeating the whole house, because she was determined to make his dinner jacket look as good as new.

At dinner they were waited on by a butler in white gloves. All the male guests were doctors, doctors who, needless to say, referred their patients to the master of the house.

Mandalin resembled a rabbit. A life-size oil portrait of him wearing all his decorations hung in the place of honor in the drawing room, next to that of his handsome wife.

"Do you play bridge, madame?"

Germaine blushed and said no, as if admitting to some moral defect.

"I have so little time, you see . . . what with the two children and all the housework. . . ."

She was hard put to stop herself from sitting on the edge of her chair, calling the butler sir, and thanking him every time he handed her a dish.

"Look here, Mandalin . . ."

For just the previous day Bergelon had been invited by the surgeon to address him in this fashion.

Bergelon pointed to his watch. Madame Cosson had been admitted to the clinic that afternoon, and a telephone call had come through at eight o'clock to inform them that she was in the first stage of labor.

"Don't worry, old man. We'll be there in plenty of time."

Toward the end of dinner the butler had bent over

Mandalin and had spoken to him in a whisper. Bergelon had no doubt that the message concerned Madame Cosson. He had shot an inquiring glance across the table.

"There's nothing to worry about."

From then on it had been a nightmare. There was no sense of urgency. Bergelon was overexcited. He was unaccustomed to wearing a dinner jacket and to playing bridge for ten centimes a point. The glass of whisky at his elbow seemed to be always full. His partner—herself the daughter of a professor on the Medical Faculty—was the wife of the ear, nose, and throat man.

Mandalin danced to the music of the phonograph, bending over his partners and murmuring sweet nothings in their ears. They responded with dazzling smiles.

Bergelon would have liked to ask him whether . . . He consulted his watch. . . . His partner rebuked him for having revoked . . . Babbling incoherently, he attempted to justify himself. . . . And all the while, Germaine, alone in a remote corner of the room, watched him with a disapproving expression. She said thank you when she was offered *petits fours*. . . . She said thank you when she was offered champagne. . . . She said thank you to everyone. . . . She was all sweetness and humility.

Two hours . . . two and a half hours . . . In the meantime another telephone call from the clinic. The ear, nose, and throat man indicated that it was time to leave.

"Let's go and see how things are going, old man. Meanwhile, my chauffeur will drive your wife home."

Germaine had no doubt been unstinting in her thanks to the chauffeur.

As for Mandalin and Bergelon, they had walked to the Ville-Haute under a starry sky, breathing in the fresh air of a perfect night.

"You see, old man, if they had their way, they'd have us cooling our heels at their bedside for ten hours at a

stretch. But some days I have as many as ten operations.
... My head nurse is perfectly competent to carry out my instructions."

Was it Bergelon who was swaying on his feet? Was it Mandalin? Or was it both of them?

"At no trouble to yourself, you could earn a steady ten to twenty thousand francs a year if, from time to time, you would send me . . ."

What else had he said? Oh, yes, that he had twelve beds to fill, twelve beds that entailed the same heavy expenses whether in use or not.

They found Cosson standing at his wife's bedside, holding her hand, his lips trembling and a look of despair in his eyes.

"Tell me, doctor . . ."

"Now, listen to me. I want you out of here, the sooner the better. Go and wait on the grounds. I'll send for you when it's all over."

A broad wink at Bergelon, as if to say, "That's the stuff to give the troops!"

He glanced absently at the chart handed to him and made a show of taking the patient's pulse, swaying on his feet all the while.

"Take her to the operating room. . . . Notify Mademoiselle Berthe. . . . An injection of . . ."

They could hear the whistles of passing freight trains. Apart from the staff of the railroad station, they were probably the only people still awake in the whole town.

No, there was one other. One-eyed Hubert, the poacher, a former patient of Bergelon's who at this hour would be casting his nets in the Loire, to supply the outdoor cafés with fish for their Sunday fry.

"Are you sure, doctor, that . . ."

Cosson was expelled. Quite literally expelled. Mandalin was a formidable authoritarian. A baby wailed in a room nearby, while a nurse emerged from another room carrying an enamel bowl filled with cotton swabs.

"No change."

"What about number seven?"

"Not too good."

Mandalin was drunk, Bergelon was convinced of it, but he was also aware that he himself was drunk. There was soft lighting everywhere and flowers outside every door, flowers that had been removed from the bedrooms for the night. From time to time a bell rang and a light came on as in a hotel, patients summoning a nurse to give them a drink, to ease their pain, or simply to relieve their loneliness.

"Wait here a minute, old man."

Mandalin had addressed him by the familiar *tu*. When he reappeared he was wearing felt-soled slippers and had a red rubber apron tied around his waist. He wore a white cap on his head, and half his rabbity face was hidden behind a gauze mask.

He communicated by sign language only. He signaled his orders. And he was swaying on his feet. Swaying more and more all the time . . .

Cosson was outside on the grounds, giving full rein to his emotions over the tulips, the coming dawn, and the mysterious events of the night which were to culminate in the birth of his child.

The arrival of the stretcher . . . the adjustable table . . . the mask . . .

Bergelon, feeling stricken, had subsided into a chair in a corner. He was by now a good deal less drunk, or so he thought. He was sorely tempted to intervene, to protest that all these proceedings were farcical. There was a better and simpler way of delivering a woman of her child: his own way, the way he had delivered so many in his time.

Too many surgical instruments glittering in the enamel bowl . . . the forceps . . . Mandalin looking at him, as if to say:

"Leave it all to me! Just you wait and see."

And then, suddenly, muttering through the gauze mask:

"Hell's bells! What a bloody mess!"

It was very hot in there. The two nurses exchanged glances. They covered the face of the woman in labor. The sound of a train . . .

And then Mandalin's hand, holding the forceps, slipped. . . . Because he had been drinking . . .

He straightened up and pulled off his mask. Gasping for breath, he murmured:

"There was nothing else to be done."

The child was dead.

"Look, Bergelon, while I'm attending to things here, I'd be obliged if you'd break the news to the father. . . ."

He had struggled on for nearly another hour.

"No luck, old man. . . . Would you care for a smoke?"

They had walked back into town along deserted streets, to the sound of blackbirds singing; the white walls of the houses were gilded with sunlight. When they came to the parting of the ways, Mandalin murmured:

"I've given all the necessary instructions. . . . I hope that it will be possible to stop the bleeding. . . . My head nurse . . ."

He had eaten three croissants, never once taking his eyes off the cockerel. The clock ticked on the mantel. Germaine said:

"I promised Annie we'd take her on the river."

There were boats available for hire on the Loire, just a two-kilometer bus ride from Bugle. Annie would recline in the bow, like a grown-up lady, trailing both hands in the water, while her father, in his shirt sleeves, plied the oars in a leisurely fashion, and Germaine toted up her troubles of the past week.

"I don't know if I'll be able to make . . . I've got to go to the clinic. . . . I really must go and get dressed. . . . I'll have to hurry. . . ."

"You'll find all your things laid out on the second shelf of the wardrobe."

The bells summoning the faithful to High Mass . . . He, as a rule, preferred the eleven o'clock service, the last one, which was generally attended only by a few men standing near the door.

No matter! He washed and shaved. He lacked the energy to run himself a bath. Besides, on Sundays, after all the others had already had their baths, the water would be no more than lukewarm. He cut himself while shaving, and mopped up the blood with a face towel. He dabbed his face with powder, leaving traces behind his ears.

Was that the doorbell? Who could it be? Germaine went to answer it. She ushered someone into the waiting room, with the green armchairs.

He did not hear her come up the stairs. He never did. She crept about, making no sound. She opened the door; looking pale and solemn, a messenger of doom, she murmured:

"The Cosson boy is downstairs."

He and she had both known him since his childhood, long before he grew to be a teen-ager, and later, an excitable adult. All three were natives of the same parish. They had all gone to the same schools, attended the same services in the church of Saint-Nicolas, and bought ices from the same Italian ice cream vendor.

"What did he say?"

"He wants someone to go to the clinic. . . . The bleed-ing . . ."

He was ready. He went downstairs. Averting his eyes, like a criminal, he opened the door.

He was the same with his wife. He was incapable of putting up a bold front. He behaved like a guilty man before he had been accused of anything. Why was it that —instead of blaming Mandalin, who had driven off to La Sologne with his family, as if he had not a care in the world—he felt impelled to say:

"You poor boy!"

"You must come quickly. . . . The nurse won't say anything, but I can guess. . . . I've got a taxi waiting outside. . . ."

In other words, she was dying! There was every reason to suppose that she would never leave the clinic. If poor Cosson were even to suspect what had gone on between three and four in the morning. . . .

All that was required of Bergelon was to assume a grave expression and keep his mouth shut, or at most to utter a few solemn platitudes. Instead of which, they sat side by side in the taxi, driving through their own district, looking out on the sunlit streets dappled with patches of shade. As they passed the little square, shaded by plane trees, which was used as an open market place for the sale of caged birds on Sundays, he repeated, danger-ously:

"You poor boy!"

"Do you think she . . . ?"

Was his distress genuine, or was it not? Were there tears in both men's eyes, or only in the ones that Cosson could see?

It was the last thing that Bergelon had intended. The tears welled up in spite of himself. As they drove, he noticed a large cage full of parakeets, and he had a sudden urge to keep parakeets in an aviary in his garden!

Moreover, as they passed the Italian with the ice cream cart, he experienced the taste of ice cream in his mouth, just as he had done as a child.

Feeling embarrassed, he resorted to self-justification:

"I can assure you that Doctor Mandalin and I did everything in our power to . . ."

The very last thing he ought to have said! The young man raised his head sharply, like a startled bird. He had bird-like features: bright beady eyes, sharp nose and chin, and thin lips. People of his sort were capable of anything, especially when they got carried away.

"You swore to me that the baby's position was perfect."

"One can never be sure."

"They telephoned you three times in the course of the evening, and . . ."

What was the use of worrying at this stage? They were still driving through his own district, on familiar streets. There was the grocer's, opposite the school, where they sold candy, as well as fruit and vegetables.

"I assure you, my dear boy . . ."

"The nurses won't say a word to me. It's as if they had something to hide."

They were now passing through different streets. They were more like avenues, though the trees were still too young to provide much shade. There were rows of showy villas that had cars parked at their gates. Most of the people who lived here, like Mandalin, were taking advantage of the spring weather to go for a drive in the country.

Cosson's eyes were rimmed with red. His tie was undone. He was smoking a cigarette, which he held between brown-stained fingers.

He tapped on the window to stop the driver, who had overshot the entrance. He looked at Bergelon. Bergelon turned his head away.

Why should he imagine that he could read an accusation in the eyes of his companion? If there were doubt and suspicion there, was he himself not encouraging them?

A gate. An elderly porter in hospital uniform.

"Whom do you wish to see?"

"The patient in number nine."

And the grounds . . . the hyacinths . . . the tulips . . . a hose, with the sprinkler rotating all on its own in the middle of a lawn . . . a nurse hurrying past with feeding bottles.

Jean Cosson walked with long, rapid strides. Had he dared, he would have dragged his companion along by the arm. But Bergelon, reading his mind, took the precaution of dropping back a little.

The window, which had been lighted all through the night, was now masked by a black shade.

His head was swimming again. . . . He had a foul taste in his mouth. . . . He could feel the warm sun on the back of his neck. . . .

Marthe Cosson was dead.

He averted his gaze. He stared at the Loire, which was glittering with millions of specks of light. He felt violently sick.

And the worst of it was that Cosson never ceased to watch him intently.

Chapter Two

H ello, is that you, old man?"

"Doctor Bergelon speaking," replied Elie, as he invariably did. He was fidgeting with a paper knife.

It gave him an odd feeling to be listening to Mandalin at the other end of the line, at the same time gazing at the pallid stomach of Madame Pholien, who was stretched out on the narrow, oilcloth-covered examination table.

Bergelon was taking in what was being said to him, of course. But the little half-smile on his face was due to quite other thoughts. He was reflecting that Madame Pholien, like himself, had lived all her life on Rue Pasteur. His house was number three. Hers was number twenty-seven. To all intents and purposes, she was the same elderly lady now as she was in the old days, when as a kid he used to break her windows with his rubber ball. He never dreamed then that a time would come when she would expose her stomach to him and tell him all her little troubles.

"Tell me, did you personally attend the funeral? Did he speak to you?"

Bergelon was still gazing smilingly at Madame Pholien's stomach when Mandalin's words brought him down to earth. Not with such a bump, however, that he had not had time to recall the scraping of the violin which could be heard whenever one went past the Pholiens', for Madame Pholien's husband, who had a wild mop of hair, had been a music teacher. Come to think of it, hadn't Jean Cosson been one of his pupils?

"The funeral . . . Oh, yes . . . No, he didn't speak to me. . . . But, you know, there was a very large attendance."

There were even people crowding the sidewalks all along the route to see the two coffins, that of the mother and of her child. Cosson—all in black, needless to say, his eyelids and nose red and swollen, a handkerchief crumpled into a ball in his hand—stared straight ahead with a wild look in his eyes. He was being supported by an uncle, who kept a firm grip on his arm.

Bergelon, like everyone else, had shaken his hand at the gate of the cemetery, and, like everyone else, had received a little nod in reply, a silent expression of thanks from the brokenhearted widower.

The cockerel was crowing at the bottom of the garden. From Halkin the blacksmith's workshop could be heard the sound of heavy hammer blows on metal, a sound that echoed through the entire parish. Madame Pholien, while pretending not to listen, was trying to hear what was being said. And Bergelon was still fidgeting with his paper knife, which was a souvenir of Lourdes.

"He hasn't been to see you since?"

"Not yet."

Mandalin gave a little cough, then paused to speak to one of the nurses who had come in to ask him about something. The sun was shining everywhere—up there at the clinic, hot and blazing; beating down on the flower beds on the grounds; and into Bergelon's consulting room, the windows of which overlooked the street. There was sunshine, too, or rather a flood of vibrant light and a rumble of sound, engulfing the parish church of Saint-Nicolas.

"Are you still there? . . . Listen, old man . . . I had them send him a bill for the fees, in the usual way . . . and I've just noticed it lying here on my desk. . . . He's returned it to me unopened. . . . I thought I'd better warn you, just in case . . ."

In case Bergelon had any thought of claiming the commission that Mandalin had promised him! Mandalin was worried. Madame Pholien brushed away a fly that had settled on her stomach. This was the third time she had come to get him to examine it, being convinced that she had a grumbling appendix.

"And that's not all. . . . My head nurse has just told me that he's been bothering one of the other nurses, the little redhead that you saw when you were at the clinic. He stopped her in the street and asked her all sorts of questions. Do you see what I'm getting at?"

For the second time Bergelon felt a jolt, as he had the previous Sunday morning when he had awakened with a hangover. It was as if a brake had been released. He clenched his hand on the paper knife. It seemed to him that the ties that bound him to his consulting room, to the street where he lived, to his own little world, had suddenly been loosened.

"There's nothing we can do about it, is there? I just

thought I'd better let you know, in case he comes by to see you."

By a strange coincidence, at that same moment Bergelon caught sight of someone through the window, whom he recognized as Jean Cosson. A few seconds later the front-door buzzer sounded. For the door was not kept locked during office hours. The patients had merely to push it; the door would open and activate the buzzer. Germaine ascertained, by looking out of the kitchen window, that the caller was for her husband and that she need not trouble to go to the door. The patients would make their own way into the waiting room and remain there until it was their turn to be seen.

"When will I be seeing you?"

"Soon."

Bergelon was worried. Many of his patients called him "the little doctor," partly because most of them had known him since he was a kid, partly because at the age of thirty-three he did not look a day over twenty-five, and partly because he really was small, slight, and sprightly.

"I'm sorry about that," he said to Madame Pholien as he replaced the receiver.

Then he proceeded to probe her stomach with his fingers.

"Breathe in. . . . Hold it. . . . Does this hurt? . . . And this? . . . Do you feel it more on one side than the other? . . . I can assure you that you haven't got appendicitis . . . just a slight inflammation of the bowel, that's all. . . . I'll give you a prescription, and I want you to take the medicine every morning before breakfast for the next few days. . . ."

"That was about Cosson, wasn't it? I wonder if it's true, what I was told yesterday. . . . He looked so very unhappy! I still remember him as he was when he used to come to the house for violin lessons."

While she was getting dressed, he wrote out the prescription. She went on talking. She had a monotonous voice that sounded to him like the buzzing of a wasp.

"According to my information, he's been carrying on for ages with a licensed prostitute...."

He looked up in surprise. She went on:

"Do you think that can possibly be true? A young man who has been married barely a year—and to such a gentle, unassuming little thing."

She folded the prescription and put it in her bag. Then, remarking, as she always made a point of doing, that getting into debt was against her principles, she put her twenty francs down on the desk.

Bergelon opened the door. Madame Pholien went out, sweeping past those waiting in the dim anteroom. The doctor had no need to say, "Next, please."

The next patient was already on her feet and going into the consulting room. The doctor glanced quickly at the most recent arrivals.

"It's my little girl, doctor.... For two days now, she's had spots on her back and chest...."

A cart rumbled past on the street.

Bergelon struggled to prevent his mind from straying back to the Cosson problem. He did not succeed. He wished he could shrink into himself, as one huddles into a warm coat.

For he was, by temperament and habit, withdrawn and solitary; often, when Germaine was talking to him about some grave domestic issue, she would interrupt herself, puzzled and vexed to observe an absent smile on his face, to ask:

"What is it? What's on your mind?"

Nothing. He wasn't thinking of anything in particular. He was listening to the bustle of life on the streets, to sounds—some of them a long way off, two blocks away, on Place Gambetta, where the market was held. The sounds of the market brought back the smells of his childhood: he and his mother had threaded their way among the stalls, the baskets of fruit and vegetables, and the thick wedges of pie, sold by one of the old market women, that always made his mouth water.

"It's unwholesome. . . . Who knows what she puts in it?"

Mingled with the other sounds were the noises of children at play outside his own school on Rue de la Loi, where he had been one of the privileged few who were permitted to spend their free time weeding the flower beds in the headmaster's garden.

All the same, he was not deaf to what his wife had been saying: her contemptuous comments on his patients had not escaped him.

"I was wondering if it could be measles, doctor. One of my neighbor's children has it."

"No, it's nothing like that, my dear. It's just a slight heat rash, nothing more serious than that. All you need to do is apply talcum powder, plenty of talcum powder."

Next! Cosson was still waiting to be seen after all the others had gone. He was not reading. He was wearing his mourning suit and holding his hat, which was trimmed with a crepe band. Every time Bergelon opened the door, Cosson looked up and fixed the doctor with his piercing gaze.

In fact, he was not quite as young as he seemed. If Bergelon was not mistaken, he had been in his first year at school when Bergelon had received his school certificate, in which case he must be twenty-six or -seven. . . . Hadn't he had a brother who had died while doing his military service?

"Next!"

He was growing impatient. One of his patients, Thioux

—who had ceased to address him by the familiar *tu* since he had qualified as a doctor, although they had played together as children in the streets—was looking at him in surprise, though he did not venture to make any comment. Thioux, who was a baker, had gotten a hernia by heaving sacks of flour about his premises.

Germaine, who had been waiting for Thioux to leave, hastened to bring Bergelon his daily cup of tea before the next patient was called into the consulting room.

"Have you seen who is out there in the waiting room?"

"Yes, of course! What of it?"

The children had just returned from school, and Emile, as usual, was dawdling in the hall.

Now there was only one left. Only Cosson. As he rose to his feet Bergelon, in spite of himself, clenched his fists.

"Good afternoon, doctor."

He was more than a man in the grip of anguish, he was anguish incarnate. He felt impelled to color even that commonplace greeting with overtones of the deepest tragedy. No sooner was he close enough for Bergelon to smell his breath than it was apparent to the doctor that he had been drinking.

"Take a seat. What's the trouble?"

"Oh, I'm not ill, if that's what you're thinking! I'm not here on my own account. . . ."

His whole manner grated on Bergelon. His tone of voice did not ring true. His glance, at once furtive and aggressive, wandered over the undistinguished furnishings of the consulting room, as if seeking God alone knows what incriminating clue.

"It's about Marthe. . . . I can't get her out of my mind. . . . Last night I didn't sleep a wink. . . . I lay awake, thinking, for hours. . . ."

He was very thin. His eyes were sunken. His hair was

too long. He had the habit of cracking his knuckles; every time he did it, Bergelon gave a start.

"To begin with, I can't understand why I wasn't allowed to be present for the birth."

He was entitled to some sort of answer. But why did Bergelon's voice sound false to his own ears? Why was he fidgeting with his paper knife again? Why, instead of sitting at his desk, was he pacing up and down his consulting room and repeatedly glancing out the window?

"It's a rule of all medical establishments. Unless the father makes a formal application in writing, accepting full responsibility . . ."

"And what about the doctor? Has he no responsibilities?"

His tone was harsh and his lips were trembling.

"Why did Doctor Mandalin not come at once in response to the nurse's telephone call?"

"Because it would have been premature at that stage."

This was a grave blunder! He had no business sounding as if he was lying or prevaricating. For that was how he did sound, and he knew it, which only made matters worse.

"You must understand, my dear boy . . ."

Why say "my dear boy" when he knew full well that he was incapable of tossing it off lightly, as Mandalin and his kind did when addressing all and sundry as "old man"?

"To begin with, I'm not your 'dear boy,' I'm your patient."

"That is so."

"As your patient, I have a right to know. I have the feeling that the truth is being withheld from me, that from the very start I haven't had a straight deal. Can you, in all conscience, assure me that I am mistaken?"

Now, when it was incumbent upon him to speak, the doctor remained silent.

"The nurse telephoned three times. I was just outside the door. I didn't hear everything, but I do know that she told the doctor it was urgent."

"You don't understand; you couldn't be expected to. It's the responsibility of the specialist to evaluate his patient's condition and to judge in advance precisely when his intervention will be needed."

"And to arrive too late!"

"Of course not! What on earth makes you think he arrived too late?"

"The child is dead. . . . And besides, I was told a lot of lies. . . . I asked one of the nurses. . . . I now know there was nothing organically wrong with the baby. . . ."

Bergelon felt cold, cold through and through. He flung the paper knife down on the desk. It was serving no purpose but to make him even more nervous than he already was.

"These tragic mishaps do occur."

"Tragic for whom?"

"For everyone concerned, I assure you."

He felt cold, and yet he was perspiring. There was a faint, lingering taste of whisky in his mouth. He could see himself seated at the bridge table, anxiously looking at his watch, lacking the courage to importune Mandalin with his sense of urgency. What had he been doing there among all those prosperous city doctors? And his wife, too, crouching in a corner, ashamed of the hands that were chapped and roughened with housework.

"When I think that Marthe . . ."

Cosson sniffed and averted his gaze, not so much to hide his tears as because it was the proper way to behave when weeping in the presence of someone else.

Then suddenly, without warning, he stood up straight,

and the doctor realized for the first time that he was a head taller than himself. With the tears still running down his cheeks, he went on in a broken voice:

"It isn't your wife who is dead, is it? If it had been his wife in labor, do you think your precious Mandalin would have left it until the very last minute? And another thing: Why were you both wearing dinner jackets? What were you doing while Marthe and I were waiting for you to arrive? And when you did arrive, you, yes, you yourself, were puffing away at a big cigar, and it didn't even occur to you to put it out or throw it away before going into the sickroom."

It was true. Bergelon had forgotten about it until now. He never smoked cigars!

"But I mean to get at the truth. . . . I don't care how long it takes. . . . If you are responsible for the death of my wife and child, I will find out. . . ."

He groped for his hat; he had difficulty finding it because his eyes were misted with tears.

"There, I've said what I came to say. You're welcome to repeat it to your friend Mandalin. As for his bill, I might as well tell you that I sent it back to him without even opening the envelope. It's not that I care about the money. That means nothing to me any more. I did everything, everything in my power, to ensure that all would be well. Now I spend hours wandering around in the street, because I can't face going back to an empty house. . . ."

How should Bergelon have reacted? He just sat there motionless, his head drooping.

His visitor, having at last found his hat, sneered as he opened the door to leave:

"It's no hardship, is it, to play havoc with other people's lives?"

The door slammed. Outside, Cosson stood hesitating

for a moment on the sidewalk, mopping his face and putting on his hat, apparently undecided where he should go.

Germaine chose this inopportune moment to put in an appearance.

"What did he say?"

She could hardly have sounded more woebegone! What on earth had possessed him to marry a woman who seemed to anticipate every conceivable misfortune that life could offer, who spent her days sighing and resigning herself to troubles that had not yet befallen her?

She was the daughter of a shopkeeper who had sold heating stoves and gas appliances on Rue Saint-Nicolas. Bergelon and she had played together as children. Even then she had been more often sad than cheerful. At the time he had found this rather touching.

He recalled, among other things, a small, dead bird, which she had buried at the edge of the Loire. The grave was surrounded by pebbles and branches, turning it into a kind of miniature cemetery.

How old had they been when they had taken to exchanging kisses in corners after dark, especially in the shadow of the school walls, where the lighting was very dim? Sixteen?

They had been fond of each other in a quiet way, like an old married couple. It was as if their union had been preordained from time immemorial.

And when he came back to Bugle, having completed his studies, there she was, wearing a broad-brimmed straw hat trimmed with blue ribbon. (It was probably still around, somewhere up in the attic.)

By then Bergelon was on his own. His father had recently died, one night when he had been even more drunk than usual. His mother had gone to live in the country, a few miles from Bourges, where she was born.

It was the day of the church festival. There were stalls and shooting galleries. Germaine was wearing a white dress, graceful in all her movements, he thought, as light as a feather.

As before, they had retreated to a dark corner and exchanged kisses, and three months later they were married.

He was not unhappy. He could not truthfully say that he was. Besides, he was incapable of unhappiness; there were always so many small, private things that gave him pleasure.

His son Emile, he thought, probably resembled him in this. He was not absolutely sure, because he was too reserved to talk of such matters, but every now and then he noticed a sparkle in Mile's eyes, a fleeting expression of delight on his face. The boy listened. He savored his surroundings. He allowed the unobtrusive, barely perceptible qualities of inanimate objects to permeate his consciousness.

"What are you thinking about, Mimile?"

Germaine called him Mimile. Bergelon called him Emile or Mile.

"Nothing, Mother."

And that was another odd thing. Mile always addressed his mother as Mother, but he called his father Daddy.

Bergelon crossed to the window and looked out on the sunlit cobbled street, thinking of the old days; weeds used to grow between the paving stones and had to be pulled up from time to time. The ditch was still there, where he used to play marbles.

Germaine, perhaps a little more faded than in her first youth, but still much as she had always been, came into the room, prepared, as usual, for the worst.

"What did he say?" she whispered.

He pondered a suitable reply, could think of none, and snapped crossly:

"Nothing!"

"You haven't drunk your tea."

"So what?" he retorted, working himself into a rage. "What if I haven't drunk my tea? It's not the end of the world!"

Between the lot of them, they had darkened his horizons and snatched away his little private pleasures, which he had thought to be inviolable and had been striving in vain to recapture.

"He must be dreadfully unhappy!"

"Dreadfully."

"I can hardly bear to think of it. . . . That poor boy, so good, so hard-working. His mother sacrificed everything to give him a decent education. It's even crossed my mind that he might do something foolish. . . ."

She lacked the courage to call a spade a spade. By "something foolish," she in fact meant suicide.

But Jean Cosson had not committed suicide. Instead, he was behaving like a man possessed. He was pursuing a very strange course. Where could it lead him in the end?

In this connection, Bergelon was reminded of something Madame Pholien had told him—namely, that Cosson was involved with a licensed prostitute. Could there be any truth in that?

If only he could rid his mind of Cosson! Had Mandalin spared a thought for Cosson since he had telephoned his colleague to warn him that he was unlikely to receive the fee that had been promised him? Had Mandalin taken the trouble to attend the funeral? Would he even recognize Cosson if he met him in the street?

Admittedly, Mandalin was not a native of the area. He had set up practice in Bugle quite fortuitously, simply because after extensive inquiries here and there it had seemed a suitable place in which to set up a profitable surgical and maternity clinic.

He lived in a large period house with a carriage gateway, on a square shaded by plane trees. It was surrounded by other houses of similar character, in an atmosphere of such forbidding, aristocratic silence that no child was ever seen to play there.

"Do you have any more visits to make this evening?"

"Possibly . . . yes."

Why was she incapable of understanding that there were times when it was her duty to remain silent? What could he say to her, since he himself did not know the answer?

"Annie is going to dinner with the little Mabille girl. She wants to know whether you'll be able to bring her home afterward."

"Of course!"

There was no point in making an issue of it. It was now five o'clock. He had one visit to make, on the waterfront, next to the cooper's, where an old man lay dying all alone in the dimly lit garret to which he had been confined for the previous ten years.

As a rule, he looked forward to these visits. He loved the waterfront and the house where the old man lived, which had once been a farmhouse. Over the years the town had gradually engulfed most of the land, leaving only a few low outbuildings; a yard with a dunghill, a few empty barrels, and some hens; and an orchard, where for a few cents the local housewives were permitted to hang out their laundry.

He did not go in. The old man, whose name was Hautois, would have to manage without him for once.

He was deeply troubled, but not on account of the dead woman, not even on account of the child. Because of Jean Cosson, was it?

No, or at least only marginally. The real trouble lay within himself: he was in turmoil. It was as if he was incubating some disease, and the symptoms were only beginning to become apparent.

He prowled the streets. He exchanged greetings with everyone he met, for he was known to everyone.

He knew every house and everyone who lived in it. He knew the family history of every resident. To his left, two blocks ahead, was the girls' school where Germaine had been educated. On the street beyond that was the brand-new apartment, above the pork butcher's, where Cosson lived.

He walked past the building. At street level it was faced with white marble, and the two floors above were of a pleasant red brick. There was a separate entrance to the apartments, with two brass plates, one bearing the name of Cosson.

Presumably he was not at home.

A group of boys were playing in the street, at least three of them patients of Bergelon. He could tell who the others were simply by virtue of their resemblance to their parents, all of whom he knew.

Farther along, some hundred yards beyond the church of Saint-Nicolas, was the beginning of the shopping district, its narrow streets lined with tightly packed rows of little shops. Still farther along, away from the noise and bustle of grocers', butchers', and shops redolent of every kind of food, was the district where Mandalin lived.

Mandalin, who must be thinking: Poor little fellow! The first patient he's ever referred to me, and this had to happen!

Mandalin, patronizingly offering him whisky, and smiling at his blunders at the bridge table!

On the corner of Rue des Minimes, next to a theater that showed nothing but second-rate gangster films, an unwholesome little enclave had sprung up, comprising three or four small bars in a row, their walls painted a garish blue or orange. Service was provided by impudently familiar barmaids, and the people of the locality tended to avoid them. Even their names were repellent: Zanzi-Bar, Select Bar, Pally Alley. Wedged between them was a rooming house, its permanently open door revealing a dark entrance hall with a staircase at the back.

Bergelon had once been summoned there at one o'clock in the morning, to find a prostitute half dead from strangulation by a sadistic client who was a prosperous local grain merchant. Bergelon could not now remember whether the man had ever been brought to justice.

And there they were, the prostitutes, loitering in the bars and on the sidewalks. He knew them all, because he and one other doctor were responsible for carrying out the weekly hospital examination, obligatory for all licensed prostitutes.

Which one was it? He was still thinking about Cosson. He felt Cosson clinging to him, like a wet shirt after a downpour of rain. Madame Pholien had said . . .

He paused outside the theater; whom should he see in the second bar, the front of which was open to the elements, but Jean Cosson himself! The bar was the one painted orange. Cosson was standing at the counter, with a small glass of spirits in front of him. He was leaning forward and talking to the barmaid, feverish as ever, tense and vehement, with a lock of his mousy hair flopping over his forehead.

What business was it of his? thought the little doctor. All he had to do was turn back and go home. There might well be an urgent telephone message awaiting him. The postmistress was suffering from a duodenal ulcer, which was liable to burst at any time. After dinner he had promised to pick up his daughter, who at thirteen was invited out to dine like a grownup, and who was never so happy as when she was allowed to entertain her friends at afternoon tea.

Cosson turned around, glanced up and down the street, and caught the doctor's eye.

No doubt he was drunk. He sniggered, pointed at Bergelon, and began talking more volubly than before to the barmaid, who had a long scar on her neck.

In every respect, Bergelon had done precisely those things that he should have avoided. Seeing the young man turn to look at him once again, he reluctantly moved away, feeling embarrassed. As he walked past a shop that sold hats, he remembered that he had left his gray hat there to be cleaned. He did not have the heart to go in and be subjected to a harangue on politics from the proprietor, who had twice stood for election to the Town Council and had twice been defeated.

He walked on, thinking of Cosson—he could not get him out of his mind. And the thought of Cosson somehow triggered memories of his own father; suddenly, for the first time in his life, it occurred to him to wonder what had driven the man to drink.

Bergelon senior had been a heavy drinker. He drank alone, any time, anywhere, even in bars such as those adjoining the theater. He would empty the little glasses at a single gulp, absently wiping his reddish beard with the back of his hand.

He hardly ever spoke. He was never unsteady on his feet. The remarkable thing was that many of his patients stayed with him. These were the ones who would say:

"Even when he's dead drunk, he never makes a wrong diagnosis."

There may have been some truth in that. He had a remarkable understanding of the human body, of the flesh and all its ills. He would declare brutally:

"You stink, my friend!"

He would say to a patient:

"You are undoubtedly going to die. And about time, too, don't you think, after all the trouble you've caused others?"

And his father before him had also been a drunkard, a cattle merchant, a conspicuous figure at every fair for miles around.

The double-fronted shop on his left, which sold heating appliances, was the one owned by Germaine's parents. As he went past he caught a glimpse of his mother-in-law at the back of the shop, arguing with a woman who was accompanied by two children.

The truth was that he was feverish. As if he were one of his own patients! But there were no signs, as yet, of any identifiable infection. He was, to use a favorite expression of Germaine's, out of sorts. He felt ill at ease. It was as if something inside him had snapped, although he could not have said what.

The sun was setting, suffusing the brick upper floors of the buildings with a deeper red. Crossing a road, he glanced down one of the side streets and saw that it was aglow like a charcoal fire.

He had only to get on with his own life and let the rest look after itself. To hell with Cosson! To hell with him! Maybe he would spare a thought for him from time to time, late at night when he could not get to sleep, but in the morning life would resume its normal course.

Once and once only, he had ventured beyond his own parish into the world of Mandalin and his kind. It had proved a disastrous failure, as he should have known it would.

As he walked on, the streets became wider and less crowded. He was home, in his own district. Except for a few new houses, it had not changed since his birth.

He caught sight of his son, gazing at the window display of a candy shop opposite his school. It gave him an odd feeling to see Mile all alone on the deserted street, standing motionless, contemplating the mounds of toffees, sugared almonds, and chocolates.

It was inevitable that they should meet. Mile, hearing footsteps behind him, turned around, started, and blushed. He had a parcel in his hand.

"I've just been to get some butter," he explained.

"Would you like some candy?"

"No, thanks."

He did not want to appear to be scrounging. His father let the matter drop.

They walked on together. Mimile put his hand in his father's. At the very end of the street was the river front, with its double row of elms, its railings, and, beyond, its steep grassy slope down to the Loire.

Dusk was beginning to darken the trees and grass. The paving stones rang beneath their feet. Mile quickened his step to keep up with his father's longer stride.

When it came down to it, what had really happened? The rhythm of life had not changed. On his right, a pork butcher's, empty of customers. On the floor above, an empty apartment.

As the light faded all the turmoil of the day was stilled. The solemnity of the moment silenced even Mile, for he too, no doubt, was moved by their shared solitude under the evening sky, which was now changing to a pale, unearthly green.

Awkwardly, Bergelon asked:

"What is your mother giving us for dinner?"

And the boy, scampering beside him so as not to be left behind, replied:

"When I last saw her, she was washing spinach."

Chapter Three

*E*very Wednesday they could be seen setting forth
in ones and twos, picking their way among the street
cleaners and the housewives who were returning home
from their morning shopping. The lowest of them, who
never ventured out of doors by day at any other time,
wore blood-red lipstick and gaudy silk blouses, and sometimes, being only half awake, shuffled along in pink or
pale-blue slippers. There were others who were simply
and neatly turned out, with sleekly stockinged legs, carrying handbags and wearing stylish hats.

They were all heading in the same direction, toward
the outskirts of the town, where there flowed a tributary
of the Loire flanked by a wide boulevard.

This boulevard, as broad as a parade ground, was
planted with six rows of trees; they were chestnuts, so

old, so tall, with such dense and spreading foliage that the buildings, glimpsed at the end of a long, seemingly converging double line of tree trunks dappled with sunlight and shade, looked like dolls' houses.

On one side, running the whole length of the boulevard, was the green fence that surrounded the hospital grounds. Once a month a horse-trading fair was held there, filling every nook and cranny. At all other times small groups of army recruits in combat uniforms could be seen there, being drilled by their sergeant.

On Wednesdays the women filed past. They were well known to the soldiers and to their N.C.O.'s. And beneath one of the trees was an old woman with her wares spread out on a folding table: slices of pie glazed with golden caramel, brioches, and cigarettes sold singly.

Every Wednesday, very early in the morning, Doctor Bergelon rounded the corner on his big-wheeled bicycle. The task of examining the prostitutes was shared between two local doctors, in practice the two most down-at-the-heel, since the local authority paid a mere pittance for each visit. The payment was fixed at two francs per capita.

What is more, the other doctor had reserved for himself the brothels; because these were house visits, the occupants had to pay an additional fee.

Bergelon's girls were the streetwalkers. The premises allotted to him were in a mean little building at the far end of the hospital complex, on the edge of the boulevard just beyond the town boundary. This same building also housed the mortuary.

He loved the boulevard, with its giant trees and diminutive soldiers. He was also very fond of the big, bare, whitewashed office, with its unfinished wood tables, its few nickel-plated and enamel instruments, its thick film of dust, its atmosphere of bureaucratic muddle, and its

Superintendent, Monsieur Grosclaude, with his big mustache and evil-smelling, swan-necked pipe.

"All going smoothly?"

"Everything's fine."

The Superintendent of the Vice Squad had a second feather in his cap. He was one of the finest billiards players in France and had represented his country as far afield as Amsterdam, Zurich, and London.

The girls strolled in, chatting unconcernedly among themselves, for they felt at home in these surroundings. They stripped for Bergelon without the least embarrassment, remarking, when the occasion arose:

"That's nothing to worry about. It's only a boil!"

And Grosclaude, ticking off the names in the register, would call out:

"See here, Maria. Do me a favor and tell Bébert that she was seen getting on the train to Paris. . . . If it happens again, I shall have to report her."

There were about half a dozen girls in Bugle who were under a restricted travel order that forbade them to go to the capital.

"She had a phone call from her sister, who is expecting a baby."

"Baby or no baby, see that she gets the message. As for you, old girl, if I ever catch you drunk and snatching the hats off people's heads, I'll revoke your license. Get it?"

He scolded them like naughty children. Their dresses lay piled in a heap. Some of them had to strip to the skin, and their underclothes were flung untidily onto an old schoolroom bench.

"Does the name Cosson mean anything to you?"

"I know lots of *cochons,* you can be sure of that!" replied the girl, with a coarse laugh. "This Cosson of yours, what's he look like?"

"Thin, very young, with long hair."

The Superintendent glanced up at the doctor. What an idiotic blunder! And it was so absolutely pointless. Indeed, if it did have any effect, it could only be to draw attention needlessly to Bergelon's uneasy sense of being in an equivocal position, and to reinforce his own inability to change the direction of his thoughts. Earlier on he had taken Grosclaude aside and told him:

"As I understand it, one of those girls is involved with Jean Cosson."

"The one whose wife died, you mean?"

One of the women, in reply to his question, said:

"Long hair? No, I haven't seen anyone like that around."

Standing beside the door was a tall girl, wearing a navy suit with a white blouse and a stylish white hat.

"You're not the one, by any chance, are you, Cécile?" the Superintendent called across to her.

"Why do you ask? What's he done wrong?"

So this was the girl!

"Nothing at all . . . I'm just interested, that's all. What sort of person is he?"

She shrugged.

"What sort of person do you think he is?"

It was a fair question. Bergelon was the one who was not thinking straight.

"Have you known him long?"

"He's more a friend than anything else."

"You mean you don't charge him?"

"That depends . . ."

She really was exceptionally tall, at least half a head taller than the rest. She was probably about twenty-three or twenty-four years old. She was very self-possessed.

"Doesn't your man object?"

"You know very well he's in Poissy."

She handed over her card to be checked and submitted to the examination with an air of dignified detachment. While Bergelon was bending over her, she looked up at him, frowning, as if she had just realized the significance of the Superintendent's questions. Noticing this, the doctor felt a twinge of uneasiness.

Really, the whole thing was too ridiculous, but then he had done so many ridiculous things in the past few days. Nothing too obvious as yet, nothing to attract attention to himself, but silly things like hovering in the vicinity of the Zanzi-Bar at times when he knew Cosson to be inside leaning on the counter.

What business was it of his if Cosson had taken to drink? What was it that drove him to catch the young man's eye, to make himself a target for the malevolent glare, full of suspicion and defiance, that was directed at him across the street?

Even now, his business completed, he did not mount his bicycle and set off on his rounds, as he should have done. Instead, he walked down the boulevard pushing his bike, accompanied by the Superintendent, who walked with long, slow, even strides.

"She's a decent, honest girl, originally from the Berry region, I think. I should have checked with her file. Her lover is serving a five-year term for having knifed a man to death in a brawl. She's not much given to picking up men on the street. She has a nice little place of her own, above a shoemaker's on Rue des Minimes. The men who visit her are mostly regulars. Nonetheless, she does occasionally take to the streets, though she has no regular beat."

The soldiers, now off duty, were crowded around the woman who sold pies and brioches. An ambulance drove out through the gates of the hospital. It was very hot.

"She's rather a pretty girl," remarked the Superintendent of the Vice Squad, in conclusion.

This was not altogether an apt description. Her figure was almost mannish, with broad shoulders, narrow hips, and underdeveloped breasts. But she had a good complexion, her skin fine-grained and smooth.

As for her face, her features were commonplace enough, except for her eyes, which were a deep amber color; when she was animated they seemed flecked with gold. But for those eyes, the doctor would scarcely have noticed her.

Why had she frowned on seeing Bergelon? Was it because Cosson had spoken to her about him? If so, what had he told her?

The two men reached the corner of the boulevard, where the town proper began. They shook hands. The doctor mounted his bicycle, undecided about which of his patients to visit first.

He was back on his own home ground. He exchanged greetings with numerous acquaintances. He could put a name to everyone he saw. All the sounds and smells of the street were familiar to him, and he knew in advance exactly where on the street the aroma of roasting coffee beans from the Epicerie Nivernaise would come wafting out to him.

What was she thinking? Cosson, a married man, had seemed so passionately absorbed in his family life. What could have induced him to become her lover?

Bergelon wished he could visit her in her "nice little place," as the Superintendent had called it. The phrase called to mind an earlier and rather turbulent period of his life, when he had been a student in Poitiers. And . . . Now it was his turn to frown, remembering something long forgotten: at that time he, too, had worn his hair somewhat longer than most of his contemporaries. He had been one of a little group who used to gather in a dimly lighted café behind the police headquarters. Among this group were two who, openly and perfectly amicably, had shared the same mistress, a tall, placid girl, not unlike Cécile.

"Which one of you will be staying tonight?" she would ask, yawning and turning down the bed.

The friend had subsequently enlisted as a naval surgeon. The woman's name was Elise, Elise Noireaud, but she was generally known only by her first name.

"I've been wondering, doctor, whether it would be safe to give him a bite to eat? He never stops complaining that he's hungry."

A little fellow five years old, lying in bed, flushed and bright-eyed.

"Give him a little weak vegetable soup, very weak."

He went from house to house. He was familiar with the furnishings of each bedroom and the individual smell of each kitchen, where he usually went to wash his hands.

The sun was climbing in the sky. The streets were full of people, cycling home from work for their midday meal. A group of house painters, covered in whitewash, were sitting on the curb, eating their sandwiches. One of them had a grudge against Bergelon, because the doctor had refused to sign a fraudulent insurance claim after an accident.

Arriving home, he wheeled his bicycle into the hall. His wife, having heard him come in, called out into the garden:

"Come in, you two! Lunch is ready. Don't forget to wash your hands, Mimile."

Even then, seated at his accustomed place in the dining room, with Emile on his left and Annie on his right, he did not feel quite his usual self. The odd thing was that he felt no pain. Often, the wife of a patient would remark, with womanly intuition, as she led him upstairs:

"I've thought for quite some time that he was getting sick."

And his own wife, no doubt, had some such thought in mind as she glanced at him uneasily from time to time. Although she, of course, could always be relied upon to expect the worst.

"Doctor Mandalin telephoned a short while ago."

"What did he want?"

"He didn't say. He's going to call again."

He ate his mutton chop and fried potatoes, to the accompaniment of some endless story that Annie was telling her mother and to which he did not bother to listen. Then, suddenly, something clicked. There was the sound of a car turning into the street. He knew with certainty that it would stop at his house. Indeed, he was already on his feet when the doorbell rang. The front door was kept shut, except during office hours when the electric buzzer replaced the peal of the bell.

"I'll go," he said. He wiped his mouth with his napkin.

It was Mandalin.

"I'm so sorry. . . . I see I've disturbed you at lunch. . . . I had intended to phone you, but as I was passing on my way back from the hospital . . ."

The clink of cutlery was no longer to be heard from the dining room. Germaine, no doubt, had silenced the children, hoping to be able to overhear what was said.

"Come into the office."

He shut the door.

"See here, old man, about that patient of yours . . . it's getting to be no joke!"

Why was it that Bergelon reacted to these words with something akin to satisfaction? One might almost think that he could not hear too much concerning Cosson.

Suddenly his little eyes were sparkling with contemptuous amusement at Mandalin. The man was visibly frightened. In profile especially, he looked more than ever like a rabbit, a rabbit scared by some loud noise.

"I went by the public prosecutor's office this morning. I tried to get you on the phone, but your wife told me you had gone out. . . . Incidentally, how is your wife?"

Mandalin could always be trusted to observe the conventions.

"Very well, thank you."

"My wife would be delighted if she would have tea with her one day soon. . . . What was I saying? Oh, yes . . . Brévannes, the public prosecutor, is a great friend of mine. I have operated on his wife and his daughter. . . ."

Glancing toward the door, he lowered his voice.

"That fellow Cosson is a madman, a dangerous madman! Believe it or not, he's written a long complaint to the public prosecutor, a tissue of lies, of course. He's demanding an exhumation and an autopsy, and he claims that his wife's confinement was scandalously mishandled. . . ."

Mandalin frowned, for it seemed to him that he had observed a fleeting smile on Bergelon's face.

Mandalin was not far wrong. Even if Bergelon was not actually smiling, he was certainly not in the least put off by this news. On the contrary, it was all he could do to conquer a childish impulse to exclaim:

"You don't say!"

He really was relishing the sight of Mandalin writhing on the hook. By contrast, his consulting room, shabby and dingy as it was, seemed a haven of unpretentious tranquillity.

"He gives chapter and verse, the times at which the phone calls were made, what he heard the head nurse say, all the information he wormed out of Mademoiselle

Berthe. According to him, by the time we arrived at the clinic we were both drunk. And he goes on to say—and this really does show what a vivid imagination he has—that you went into the operating room with a cigar in your mouth. . . ."

"So what?"

Was this what Bergelon had been waiting for these past few days? Was it because it had come at last that he felt so relieved?

"You seem to take it all very lightly, I must say! Admittedly, you haven't much to lose . . ."

His expression, as he looked around the office, spoke louder than words:

". . . with your sort of practice!"

Bergelon was still clutching his table napkin, stained with red wine.

"It's fortunate that Brévannes and I are friends. He knows me. I promised to let him have a statement signed by the two of us. If need be, I can get two colleagues to confirm in writing that there were no irregularities, and that will be the end of the matter. All the same, if I could lay my hands on that little toad . . ."

Bergelon was tickled by this description of Cosson, so much so that he was sorely tempted to echo the words aloud: "that little toad."

"Subject to your agreement, I will write a detailed report this afternoon. . . . Perhaps you would be so good as to come by my house to sign it; or, if you prefer, my secretary can bring it over to you."

"Whichever suits you. .   No, on second thought, have it sent here."

"I must be on my way. I have three operations this afternoon, not to mention the report! Oh, and by the way, I see no point in mentioning that you were dining with me that night, don't you agree?"

Poor Germaine! She had already turned toward the door at the sound of his footsteps. As he came in she looked up at him expecting the very worst, and there he was, smiling and looking positively sprightly.

"What is there left to eat?" he asked, resuming his seat.

"Stewed fruit. . . . There's nothing wrong, is there?"

"Why should there be?"

"I don't know . . . I thought . . ."

No, of course there was nothing wrong! Wheels were being set in motion, that was all. That was an odd thing, Cosson's writing to the public prosecutor in those terms. Mandalin had called him a little toad. But, come to think of it, he was no fool, just a little too hot-headed.

"Mimile! Go and open the door and turn on the buzzer."

It was half past one, and the patients would soon be arriving for consultation.

"Won't you have some fruit?"

It had not escaped her that he was eating with his elbows on the table, a habit for which she was always scolding the children.

"Go on, Mother, ask him!" said the boy, returning to the dining room.

"I hardly think this is the right moment," she protested.

Bergelon was puzzled.

"The right moment for what? Why shouldn't it be the right moment?"

"Mimile is never satisfied. First there was his Scout uniform. Then there was his subscription. And the next thing, he had to have a bicycle. Now, believe it or not, he wants us to buy him a tent. Apparently, all this summer the Wolf Cubs are going camping every Saturday in the Méran woods."

"Well?" said Bergelon, wondering what all the fuss was about.

"Don't you think he's too young to . . . ?"

"Lots of them are younger than I am! There's even one seven-year-old girl coming with all us boys!"

"Let him have his tent."

Since the buzzer had just sounded, he lit a cigarette, rolled up his table napkin, slipped it into its wooden ring, and went into the office.

Years ago, he recalled, he had had a providential stroke of luck. How old had he been, exactly? He was in the fifth grade at the lycée. His father never bothered to ask about his marks. That was the year he discovered the novels of Alexandre Dumas, and he would read as many as two a day, on the way to school. His classwork was sketchy, to say the least, and he was learning nothing.

By the beginning of June it was clear to him that he was about to fail his exams. However, although he would be stricken with acute panic several times a day, he could not bring himself to renounce Dumas.

Then, four days before the examinations were due to begin, he suddenly developed a fever, and his fears were forgotten. He woke up one morning with a temperature of 105. The next day his father diagnosed paratyphoid.

The first, critical phase was followed by a month of sheer bliss, during which he was confined to his room with nothing to do but read. He lost weight. He grew very weak. He was such a pitiful object to behold, even after he had begun to convalesce, that when examination time came around in October, he was treated with the utmost indulgence.

"What's the trouble, Madame Barmat?"

"It's about a medical certificate for my husband. He couldn't get out of bed again this morning. He still has those dreadful stomach pains. . . ."

This was a lie. Her husband had nothing at all the matter with him, but he had decided to repaint the whole inside of his house, while continuing to draw his salary.

"Give me the form."

He signed it. Just yesterday he would have refused to do so. He summoned the next patient, and the next. He seemed that afternoon to be floating on air, as when he had run a temperature of 105. Nothing seemed to matter very much any longer. He scarcely noticed the hammering coming from Halkin's workshop or the familiar sound of children shouting in the school playground.

Germaine brought him his cup of tea and crept out again on tiptoe. She always would slink in and out of the waiting room in this furtive way, as if apologizing to the patients for her existence.

Was Cécile, at this hour, receiving men in her lodgings over the shoemaker's? He was not quite sure exactly where she lived. None of his patients lived on Rue des Minimes, and he seldom had occasion to go near it. It was not far from the theater, a little short of the bridge.

"I've been taking milk of magnesia."

"Patent medicines won't do you any good. You'll just have to cut out all those apéritifs."

Another certificate, this time for a kid with mumps who had to be kept home from school.

The last patient. The last prescription. Twenty francs. Some of them had the money already clutched in their hands as they sat in the waiting room; they would put it down on the edge of the desk as soon as they entered the consulting room.

He could now shut the front door. The children were back from school.

"Elie! You surely haven't forgotten Annie's dental appointment!"

He had forgotten it, but it was of no importance.

"Is Annie ready?"

"She's brushing her teeth. She'll be down in a moment."

He went out, accompanied by his daughter. The Saint-Eloi district was some distance away.

"Now that you're going to buy a tent for Mile, what are you going to give me?"

It would not be true to say that he had no affection for his daughter, but he certainly derived no pleasure from her company. She counted every penny and saved out of her pocket money. When she talked about her little friends she was like a grown woman gossiping; what was more, Annie was already something of a social snob. She would never dream of going to school without her gloves, for instance.

The dentist was an old friend. While Annie was having a tooth filled, Bergelon prowled around the office, admiring the instruments. The dentist, meanwhile, told him of the Dental Association's decision to raise the fees.

They went out, Annie clinging to his hand.

"I didn't cry, did I?" she said, very pleased with herself.

What happened next was really no fault of Bergelon's. Perhaps he was vaguely preoccupied with the thought of Cécile, for whom this was the busiest time of the day.

No, it wasn't even that. He moved through the crowd, with his daughter tugging at his hand. She stopped to look in every shop window, chattering incessantly. The sky was now overcast. All color was drained from the streets. He had not intended to go past the Zanzi-Bar but did so because that was the shortest way.

"I must remember to go in and pick up my hat," he remarked as they passed the hat shop.

At that same moment he had a feeling that something was happening. He became aware of a man striding across the road toward him, and he all but raised his arm, as if to ward off a blow.

It was all quite clear to him, and he said to himself:

"Here's Cosson, and he's going to assault me!"

And yet, this time he had not so much as glanced toward the bar. Cosson was in a highly excitable state. Quite some time before, having already tossed off several small glasses of spirits, he had announced to the barmaid, with a snigger:

"Just you wait and see!"

The streets were crowded. It was six o'clock. The sidewalk outside the theater was so packed that there was scarcely any room to get past. The doctor's first, instinctive reaction was to stride away as fast as he could, so as to avoid a scene. But it was in vain. The enemy's footsteps were closing in. An arm shot out. Bergelon hunched his shoulders.

Then he felt Cosson's hand grip his shoulder, or rather his jacket, which he jerked upward so violently that it sent a jarring shock right through the doctor's body.

"One moment, doctor!"

He was at the boiling point. He was bent on creating a scene. Little did he care that Bergelon was accompanied by his small daughter and was holding her by the hand. People in the street were beginning to turn and stare.

"Not so fast, if you please . . . I have a few words to say to you."

A woman carrying a shopping bag, from which a bunch of leeks protruded, was the first to stop in her tracks.

"Let go of me."

It was not that the doctor was a coward, but that he was still hoping to avoid drawing a crowd.

"Not before I've said what I have to say. If either of us has the right to call a policeman, I have, do you hear?"

Annie, terrified, tugged at her father's arm, whimpering:

"Come on! Let's go!"

But Jean Cosson would not loosen his grip on his other sleeve. He was the taller of the two men. Scarcely aware of what he was doing, Cosson was jerking Bergelon almost off his feet. Bergelon, keenly aware of the absurdity of the situation, felt that he was being manipulated like a puppet.

"You know what I'm talking about, don't you? My private life is nobody's business but my own. But the lives of your patients are your responsibility. . . ."

He was trembling from head to foot. Considering the state he was in, he must have been working himself up to it for hours, if not days. His speech was so slurred that some of his words were barely intelligible. The people inside the little orange-painted bar, where he had declared that they would see what they would see, had all turned out to watch the scene.

"If I ever again catch you pestering a certain person who shall be nameless, I'll smash your face in, get it?"

Passers-by within a yard of them, three yards, five yards, had stopped dead in their tracks, waiting to see whether this was going to develop into a serious fight. They now formed a circle around them.

"Let's go, Father . . . let's go!" repeated Annie, struggling to hold back her tears.

"Get it?" repeated Cosson.

Perhaps the doctor was almost as confused as his assailant. At any rate, it had not immediately occurred to him to strike a blow in his own defense. When it did, it was already too late. Cosson had stopped shaking him and had stepped backward, well out of range. He realized now what he should have done: he should have struck him full in the face with his clenched fist—a single clean, decisive blow—and then retired with dignity.

He had not done so. He had done nothing; he had said nothing. His ears were burning. Cosson hesitated, wondering whether he had made his point forcefully enough. Should he, before returning to the bar, venture some more spectacular demonstration?

"Get it?"

It was apparent that he had run out of steam. Catching sight of a police helmet some thirty yards away, he backed off, pausing only to turn and again reiterate, "Get it?"

The woman with the leeks sighed:

"He's a drunken sot!"

At this, Bergelon flushed. The remark had been intended to comfort him, which meant she felt sorry for him.

The policeman, seeing that order had been restored, checked his stride and stood still in the middle of the road. The crowd of spectators dispersed. Annie tugged at her father's arm. It was not until they reached the corner of Rue des Prêtres that she calmed down a little.

Only then did she ask, "What did he want? Who is he?"

"No one."

Until he heard himself pronounce the words he did not realize that he had said them.

"Why did he want to hit you?"

He caught sight of his reflection in a shop window. The cloth of his jacket was bunched up where the young man had grasped it, making one shoulder look higher than the other. Bergelon felt a deep sense of shame.

He should have . . . But it was too late.

"Why did he attack you?"

The streets were cheerless now that the sun had gone down, and here, where there were no more shops or market stalls, their footsteps rang out hollowly.

His inclination was to ask his daughter to say nothing to Germaine, but if he did, Annie, puffed up with self-importance, would be sure to drop mysterious hints, making things worse in the long run.

The crowning absurdity was that as they turned the corner there was Germaine standing on the doorstep. She hastened toward them, panting:

"What happened? Are you hurt?"

So she already knew! A neighbor, the barber's daughter, had been present at the start of the incident, and had lost no time in ringing the Bergelons' doorbell.

"Listen, Madame Bergelon! Your husband has been assaulted by some man on Rue Saint-Nicolas!"

She, too, was watching from her doorstep, as was another neighbor, a few doors along.

A gray pall hung over everything, a deep, monotonous gray.

"He pounced on Daddy, and he . . ."

Annie chattered on. Bergelon could not wait to get indoors, shut the door behind him, and take off his jacket, which was dragging uncomfortably around the armpits.

"Who was it? Was it Cosson?"

Germaine's tone of voice spoke volumes. Every fiber of her being proclaimed:

"I knew it! I've been expecting something like this to happen for a long time!"

Once indoors, she pressed him further:

"Are you sure he didn't hit you?"

As if he could have avoided noticing, if he had! As if he would have bothered to lie about it anyway!

"Yes, of course I'm sure!"

"He said," Annie began, "he said that if Father . . ."

Bergelon, to put an end to it, interrupted:

"He said that if I ever meddled in his affairs again, he'd bash my face in. And that's all! He's out of his mind. . . . He was drunk. . . . And now I'd be obliged if you'd leave me alone."

He slammed the door of his office and immediately felt the muscles of his face relax.

Five minutes later he was wearing the same expression as on the occasion of Mandalin's last visit. He was all but smiling.

Chapter Four

Having just finished shaving, and hearing the front door close, he came downstairs wearing his slippers and no collar, as was his wont. The children had left for school. Their mother, as usual, was taking advantage of their absence to get her shopping done. The house was empty and filled with a savory smell from something simmering on the kitchen stove. He had no need to open the door. He knew that the milk can had been put out on the step, with the correct amount of money beside it.

The first thing he did, as had been his habit for years, was to get his mail from the mailbox. It was hardly likely that it would contain anything very exciting: just notices of meetings, advertisements for pharmaceutical products, and a great many leaflets. He stuffed everything into the pocket of his jacket, and, then and there, opened the local newspaper, *Le Phare de Bugle*. He turned to page three, always less well printed than the rest of the paper, as if the ink had almost run dry, and scanned the local news with something of a professional eye. . . . Cyclist knocked down . . . car crash . . . child bitten by dog . . .

A rectangular patch of sunlight shone onto the paper through the glass panel in the front door.

According to information received, a special meeting of the Bugle and District Branch of the Medical Association was held yesterday to rebut defamatory rumors being spread by certain persons. A motion was passed expressing the complete confidence of all those present in the two respected professional colleagues under attack.

The Committee, having investigated certain complaints lodged against a surgeon and a general practitioner in this town, have issued a statement affirming that in the case under review normal procedures were followed and no irregularities occurred.

Bergelon seldom attended the meetings of the Medical Association, but he could readily imagine Mandalin's posturings at last night's meeting.

Idiotic! Completely idiotic! Typical bureaucratic bungling!

He could hear footsteps on the sidewalk, slowing down as they approached the house, then stopping at the front door. Without so much as a glance at the glass panel, the caller dropped something into the mailbox; only then, looking up, did he see Bergelon in the dim entrance hall, observing him through the iron grate, eyes wide with astonishment.

It was Jean Cosson! For an instant the two men, with the door between them, stood rooted to the spot, equally taken by surprise. Then Cosson shrugged and walked away toward the waterfront.

Bergelon took the letter from the box and went into the dining room, where his breakfast awaited him, for he always ate later than the others in the morning. He poured himself some coffee, took a crisp croissant from the dish, and placed his mail beside him on the table-cloth. Only then did he tear open the envelope.

One of these days you will be shot.

That was all. There was no need for a signature. Even if the doctor had not seen Cosson, he would have known. The odd thing was that Cosson had used the familiar *tu*, thus establishing a kind of intimacy between them.

Unhurriedly, Bergelon ate his meal and went up to the bedroom to finish dressing. In the meantime his wife had returned from the market with her shopping. When he was ready he mounted his bicycle and went out on his rounds as usual. As he passed the pork butcher's, above which Cosson lived, he noticed that the windows on the second floor were all shut.

It was an unusually peaceful day, and he savored every moment of it in little sips, especially during the morning, which was always his favorite time of day. He felt perfectly serene. He examined his patients as if he had not a care in the world. From time to time he remembered Cosson—rather as a young man in love, in the midst of his daily preoccupations, will permit his thoughts to stray sentimentally before returning to the matter at hand.

Nothing of any significance occurred, except for a telephone call from Mandalin.

"Hello. Have you seen the paper?"

Not content with addressing him as "old man," Mandalin was now using *tu*, which did not please Bergelon.

"I have."

"It had to be stopped once and for all. . . . From now

on, if he doesn't keep his mouth shut . . . How is Madame Bergelon?"

He kept away from the little orange-fronted bar, but he could not avoid going past the pork butcher's in the late afternoon. The windows were still shut, in spite of the mildness of the weather.

The next day and the day after that were equally uneventful, filled, as usual, with small, everyday activities. The only event of note was that Germaine went with Emile to buy his tent. When Bergelon saw the parcel arrive, with the canvas, the ropes, and the bamboo stakes, he could not wait to erect it then and there in the little garden; he devoted almost two hours to the task, when he should have been visiting old Hautois in his lonely attic.

He had no sense of foreboding. Time seemed to be standing still. And yet, on the third day Bergelon knew, as soon as he turned the corner of Rue des Minimes, that events were about to take a new turn.

This was the boundary of the parish of Saint-Nicolas. The character of the streets was noticeably different, no longer calm and respectable like that of his own parish; it was much more turbulent. At ground-floor level, every building was a craftsman's workshop—a decorator, an upholsterer, a plumber, a radio repairer. And there was, astonishingly, a bookshop that sold popular novels and that was also a lending library.

All the doors and windows were open. Several old people had brought out chairs and were sitting on the sidewalk. Children were playing. An acrid odor rose from the nearby stream, the familiar odor of poverty, and between the houses could be seen other little streets, even more sordid and evil smelling.

Bergelon had left his bicycle at home. He was taking

his time. At some distance he caught sight of the shoe-maker's little shop, and it gave him a start. Leaning on the window sill on the floor above was Jean Cosson, in his shirt sleeves, smoking his pipe and glancing idly up and down the street as people in that sort of neighbor-hood tend to do.

He spotted the doctor passing by, and he turned away from the window. He must have said something to Cécile, for she appeared in her dressing gown from the semi-darkness of the room, laid a hand on his shoulder, and leaned out, seeming to ask:

"Where is he?"

Cosson pointed at Bergelon with the stem of his pipe, and it looked for an instant as if he was about to accost him. But he did not speak, contenting himself with spit-ting on the sidewalk. The spittle landed with a soft plop.

On the following Sunday the whole family set out for a day in the country, to try out Mile's tent in rural sur-roundings. The air was crystal clear and filled with pleas-ant sounds, until at four o'clock there was a sudden downpour, driving the family to take refuge in a dim little village café, full of small tables at which men sat drinking large mugs of rosé wine. Annie's white shoes were stained with mud, and her straw hat was limp and shapeless. Only Mimile had remained sheltered, weather-ing the storm in his new tent.

"What if it should be struck by lightning?" sighed Germaine.

The following day, Monday, Bergelon encountered Cécile in the street quite by chance. It was about four in the afternoon when Bergelon saw her being followed by a man in his fifties. He stood watching them from the sidewalk opposite. At the corner Cécile stopped for a moment and turned around. The man must have re-sponded with a nod, for she turned onto the side street, quickened her pace, and disappeared into a hotel. Up to that moment Bergelon had not even been aware of its existence. A second or two later the man followed her inside.

In the past few days Bergelon had passed Cosson's flat at least ten times, and not once had he seen the windows open. Nor had he seen lights in any of the windows at night, although they were all unshuttered.

Secretly, he was looking forward with impatience to the following Wednesday. Nothing had changed—the tall trees on the boulevard leading to the hospital, the little groups of soldiers, the girls coming in ones and twos from the center of town, or, last but not least, Superintendent Grosclaude, with his evil-smelling pipe.

Why this fear that Cécile might not come? She arrived as always, wearing her blue suit, her white blouse, and her hat, and she sat on the bench to await her turn. Bergelon carefully avoided looking at her, and he felt embarrassed when she hoisted herself up onto the adjustable table that was used for the routine examination.

She made no attempt to avoid his eyes. On the contrary, she watched him, composed but interested, as if since her last visit she had come to regard him as something more than just the doctor assigned to examine the licensed prostitutes.

"You're all right. . . ."

He was in the grip of a strange sort of restlessness, as if the inevitable was being unduly delayed, perhaps even postponed indefinitely.

That afternoon he again caught a glimpse of Cécile, sauntering along in search of customers. He deliberately walked past the Zanzi-Bar at the time Cosson was usually to be found there; he was disappointed not to see him.

No sooner had he arrived at the house than his wife handed him a letter, addressed in handwriting that he recognized. It was possible, judging from her worried expression, that Germaine also recognized it.

"It's not stamped," she remarked. "It must have been delivered by hand. . . ."

Don't imagine for one moment that my resolve has weakened! I am prolonging the agony, and enjoying it, but I'll get you in the end.

Well, well. Why had Cosson abandoned the familiar *tu*, he wondered.

"What is it?" asked Germaine.

"Nothing . . . Just a crank. . . ."

"Show me."

It was the wrong thing to do, and he knew it. Whenever he did wrong, he was instinctively aware of it. Yielding to some inexplicable impulse to add to his wife's anxieties, he handed her the note.

"Is it from Cosson?"

"Yes."

"Tell me . . . Do you think Mandalin, that night . . . ?"

"Mandalin was drunk!"

"And so . . . ?"

"And so, he killed them, her and the child."

What could have possessed him to say such a thing, tossing it off so casually, almost as if he enjoyed saying it?

"Don't you think you have cause to fear that young man? If I were you, I would go to the police."

He felt feverish, but pleasantly so. The trivial worries of everyday life no longer concerned him. He regarded the nervous anxieties of some of his patients almost with amusement.

"No, of course you are not going to die! What do you want to die for? I'm not dead, am I?"

"You haven't got cancer!"

"What do you know about it? No one can be certain that he hasn't got cancer."

He was compelled to be forever on the move. Twice more he had gone past Rue des Minimes. The first time he had seen no one. On the second occasion he had seen Cosson, sitting near the window with a book, which he had probably borrowed from the lending library nearby.

"Doctor Mandalin telephoned. He wants you to call him back."

To hell with Mandalin! He did not call him back. On the stroke of three, while he was busy with a patient—Madame Pholien, as it happened, still fretting about her appendix—there was a timid knock at the door, which was then opened a crack. It was Germaine.

"Can you spare a moment?"

Realizing that it must be something serious, he made his excuses to Madame Pholien and followed his wife out into the hall.

"It's someone from the police. I've taken him into the living room."

He opened the door and found himself face to face with an inspector who was a stranger to him.

"I'm sorry to trouble you, doctor. A short while ago your colleague Doctor Mandalin came to see us. I daresay you can guess what it was about?"

Bergelon did not start; on the contrary, he stood very stiff and still. The inspector's manner was at once cordial and respectful, seeming to imply by his attitude that they were both on the same side of the fence.

"I take it that you, too, will wish to lodge a complaint against this fellow, Cosson. As I understand it, he used abusive language to you in public. . . ."

Bergelon shrugged, as if to say:

"It's of no importance."

"Yesterday, while Doctor Mandalin was getting out of

his car to visit one of his patients, Cosson spat in his face and uttered insults and threats. I have been making inquiries about him. . . . He has been absent for more than a week from the bank where he works. In view of his recent bereavement, the manager sent someone to his apartment to inquire after him and was told that he had not been back there even to sleep. From my own inquiries I soon discovered that he is now living with a licensed prostitute on Rue des Minimes."

Still no response from Bergelon, not so much as a nod of encouragement.

"As I explained to Doctor Mandalin, there isn't much we can do unless he commits an actual assault. Nevertheless, you yourself also have cause for complaint; in these circumstances, I am prepared to summon him to my office and remind him that under the provisions of the penal code, he could be charged with living on immoral earnings. You see my point? However, Doctor Mandalin suggested that I ought to have a word with you before proceeding further. . . ."

"I have no intention of lodging a complaint!" declared Bergelon.

"Oh?"

The inspector was disconcerted. When you favor someone with a friendly nod and a wink, the last thing you expect is a rebuff.

"I understand . . . The Superintendent also advised me to make this call. However, seeing that all is well . . ."

He reached for his hat.

"All the same, if he should give you any trouble . . ."

"In that case, I'll certainly be in touch."

No sooner had Bergelon seen the inspector to the door than Germaine pounced on him:

"What did he want?"

"Nothing."

"Was it Cosson again?"

"No, it was not!"

And he returned to Madame Pholien, who was by now fully dressed and waiting for him, as motionless and dignified as a statue.

From five to seven he was out again visiting patients. As chance would have it, at the home of one of his oldest patients, who had originally been a patient of his father's, he was invited to stay for an apéritif.

He seldom drank. Indeed, he was almost excessively abstemious, knowing what drink had done to his father. And besides, he had a very poor head for spirits, witness that night at the Mandalins'. With him one drink tended to lead to another; so after that first apéritif with his patient, he felt irresistibly impelled to go into a bar for another on his way home.

Germaine was tactless enough to remark:

"What's the matter with you? Have you been drinking?"

"I had a drink with the Chirons. What of it?"

"Nothing. . . . Are you going out again?"

He had not changed into his house slippers, as he usually did when he was spending the evening at home.

"I do have to go out again, yes."

"Will you be late coming home?"

"I don't know."

He was very tense, and his head was throbbing. He scarcely touched his dinner, and he snapped at his daughter for no reason at all.

To tell the truth, he hated this nose for trouble that was so characteristic of his wife and which, even this very evening, had warned her that there was danger afoot.

"You're not going to see *him,* are you?" she nagged, following Bergelon into the hall just as he was on his way out.

"No!"

It was, however, *him* that he was going to see! Not right away, though. It would have been better if he had. Instead, he wandered about the streets, their sidewalks tinged with bluish light from the ubiquitous fluorescent signs. He went into one of the bars. Having no particular preference, he ordered a Calvados because there happened to be a jug of it on the bar in front of him.

"The same again."

He felt a growing sense of injustice and betrayal, and at the same time a less clearly defined but more disturbing preoccupation with Cosson and his troubles. It was this sense of injustice that had had such a chilling effect on him during the inspector's visit. He sensed a conspiracy: Mandalin and the Medical Association; Brévannes, the public prosecutor, who was a friend of Mandalin's; and even the police were involved. . . .

He recalled Cosson, in his shirt sleeves, looking down from the window at the busy street below, and Cécile pacing the sidewalk for hours at a stretch.

"The same again, bartender."

He felt a nervous twitch in his knees, a kind of warning. To hell with it! He turned onto Rue des Minimes and saw that there was a light in the window. . . . He saw the curtain move and thought that he had probably been observed.

No matter. He went in and headed for the unlit staircase, feeling his way upstairs with his hand on the wall. Several times he stumbled, making a good deal of noise. A door opened, emitting a beam of light. A man stood on the landing, waiting for him.

Suddenly Bergelon was close enough to touch him. He opened his mouth, but the man spoke first:

"Come in."

It was Cosson, who was now shutting the door behind

him. And there was Cécile, wearing a housecoat, looking scared and anxious, and attempting to remove a bottle that was standing on the table.

"Leave it!" ordered Cosson harshly.

It was immediately plain to the doctor that Cosson, too, was drunk. He ran his fingers through his hair in a characteristic gesture, and his long locks fell forward across one cheek. His complexion was blotchy, pale with red patches, and his deep-set eyes were alight with a terrible glare.

"Leave it! Why should he be allowed to stay sober when I'm drunk?"

He was tall, taller than ever it seemed, in this poky little room that was lit only by a hanging kerosene lamp. In the room immediately below, the purr of a sewing machine could be heard, that being the back room of the shoemaker's shop.

"Give him a glass. . . . Fill it to the brim. . . ."

He was breathing hard and pacing to and fro restlessly, unable to stand still for a moment. He circled around the doctor, apparently pondering how best to tackle him.

"Well, aren't you going to drink it? Are you scared or something?"

Cécile's blue suit and white blouse hung from a coat hanger. The bed was made. Adjoining the bedroom could be seen a tiny kitchen, which also served as a washroom.

"Give him some more. And fill up my glass, too. Here!"

It was some cheap, unbranded spirit, which burned Bergelon's throat and made him want to vomit, especially after the Calvados.

"You may sit down. Wherever you like . . . on the bed, if that suits you. . . . Scared out of your wits, aren't you?

Of course, you have every reason to be. . . . I said I'd kill you, and so I will. . . ."

He turned angrily on the young woman, whose pale-blue housecoat was like an eerie patch of light in the dark room.

"See here, you, either sit down or get out. You know very well I can't stand you hovering over me. . . ."

Standing opposite the doctor, he tossed his head, throwing back his long hair in a gesture that was almost a nervous tic.

"What have you come here for? Come on, out with it!"

"I came to talk to you."

"To say what? Well, get on with it! You came to tell me that you didn't kill my wife and baby, is that it?"

"No."

"So you admit you killed them, you and your friend Mandalin?"

"Listen to me, Cosson. . . ."

He was groping his way, like a man in a faintly luminous fog, one of those yellow fogs that make even the most familiar surroundings seem unreal. And yet his present surroundings were not altogether unreal. There was something about the smell and flavor of this dimly lighted room which recalled the room in Poitiers, where he and his fellow student had shared the favors of Elise Noireaud: the kerosene stove, the red coverlet on the bed, the neighbor who would bang loudly on the wall from time to time, when they were making too much noise. And in those days, too, they used to drink expressly for the purpose of getting drunk.

"Listen, Cosson, I know what you think. . . ."

"I think you killed my wife and kid. . . . Am I right or am I not?"

Bergelon said, with reluctance:

"In a sense, what you say is true."

What on earth had induced him to come here? He himself no longer knew. His mind was clouded. At the same time he felt strangely clear-sighted, so much so that he was sharply aware of things that until now had puzzled him. The trouble was that he was having difficulty expressing himself. He felt as if his temples were being gripped in a vise.

"Let me try and explain. . . . It was you who insisted that your wife should go into an expensive clinic for her confinement. . . ."

"You don't say!" sneered Cosson, pouring himself another glass, then emptying it in a single gulp.

As he spoke tears poured down his cheeks—tears of drunkenness, perhaps.

The most disconcerting element was that patch of blue on a chair in the dimness of the room, Cécile, a silent and motionless presence. On the oilcloth-covered table were shreds of ham on a piece of paper, dregs of red wine in a glass, crumbs scattered about.

"You don't in the least understand why I had to do the best for her, do you?"

Suddenly his hard expression melted, his face crumpled, and he looked as if he was about to break into sobs.

"Damn it all!" he exclaimed, as if ashamed of his own outburst of feeling. "When I think that I was doing everything . . . everything!"

What was he doing? And why?

He was drinking, wiping his mouth on his sleeve, growing mawkishly sentimental.

"Do you think it was easy, growing up the son of a humble policeman? My mother went out cleaning in order to pay for my schooling. None of the neighbors knew, because she took care to find work at the far end of town. But how could you possibly understand? Still less, your friend, Mandalin! But I don't hold it against him. It's different for him. . . . But you were born in the parish, and you're one of us."

He ran his fingers through his hair. His skin was now a deathly white, blotched with red and streaked with tears.

"I did everything I was told. . . . I was a good little boy. And I hadn't so much as a few cents to buy myself a bar of chocolate. People used to give their old trousers to my mother so that she could cut them down to make shorts for me. . . ."

Dredging all this up was painful; it came from very deep down. It was like sludge—sour, bitter, with a revolting stench. His mouth twisted in disgust.

"At school I was first in the class, always first! And when I joined the bank, I was always the one who worked the longest hours. You still don't understand, I know you don't. . . Or if you do, then you must have some glimmering. . . . Look, you're a doctor, can you deny that it was on account of all that heavy work that my mother suffered from a floating kidney? I don't give a damn! Yes, the truth is that I don't give a damn what you say. . . .

"Because I know the truth—and you don't have to look at me like that. . . . Give him a drink, Cécile. . . . I won't have him looking at me like that! I'm drunk, but he's not nearly drunk enough. . . ."

Obediently, the young woman filled a glass, handed it to the doctor, and sat down again, pulling her blue housecoat together over her knees.

Cosson also took another drink, anxious to lower the temperature and happy to have a breathing space after his outburst of rage.

It was as if his hour had come, the climax toward which he had been striving slowly, patiently, and methodically. Now he had Bergelon where he wanted him, here in this room, which seemed altogether cut off from the world beyond the lowered shade.

"They could have done anything they wanted with me, do you hear? I was a good little boy . . . a fool! A credulous fool! I saved up my money . . . and I chose my wife because she seemed a cut above the other girls I knew. . . .

"I wanted to make chief cashier or assistant manager. . . . To you that doesn't seem like much, I daresay.

"What's more, you can't have any idea what it means for a young couple, just starting out, to have to furnish a home. Not only did I do a full day's work and overtime, but I also kept the books for several small businesses. . . .

"And all to earn money! To keep a respectable home; to have an apartment with a living room. So that the baby, when it was born . . . Filthy swine, all of you! Cécile, isn't there anything else to drink in the cupboard?"

And Cécile's gentle voice:

"Only some red wine."

"Give it to me!"

The doctor was forced to drink as well. It was a heavy, viscous wine, and it sickened him.

"Listen, Cosson."

It was his turn now to long to speak out, to explain himself. The longing burned in him like a fever.

"I swear to you . . ."

"Shut your trap! From now on, I'm the one doing the talking. . . . I'm the one who has the right to talk, because you, every one of you . . ."

He spat a mouthful of red wine onto the floor.

"Now everyone thinks I'm a swine because they've found out that I was in the habit of coming here even before . . . isn't that so, Cécile? What was I expected to do, I'd like to know, seeing that my wife had a horror of lovemaking? . . . Tell him, Cécile, tell him how pleasant it was for both of us, when I used to come and spend half an hour with you after working hours at the bank. And what's more, I wasn't cheating my wife out of a single cent. Cécile can vouch for that. . . . Well, yes, that first time I did pay. . . ."

He was weeping again, but as before his anguish could at any moment turn to rage.

"After that we became friends. I used to tell her everything. She was the one I talked to most about the child we were expecting. . . . I wonder now . . . Yes, I'm sure that's how it was. . . . It was Cécile who asked me if we had a good obstetrician. . . .

"You still don't see what I'm getting at? I'd have carried on as before, I'm sure of that. . . . Hadn't I had it drummed into me more than enough that honesty was the thing that mattered most?

"Whereas all of you, swine that you are . . .

"Oh, that night . . . I was sick with anxiety. . . . I couldn't keep still. . . . I felt my heart was breaking. . . . I kept repeating to my wife:

" 'Don't worry, there's nothing to fear. You are in the hands of the best surgeon in Bugle.'

"And all the while . . .

"After all, I didn't know Mandalin. He is what he is. . . . No doubt, he can't help himself. . . .

"But when I discovered that he was turning the fee for the confinement over to you . . ."

"Listen, Cosson . . ."

The doctor had risen to his feet. There was a mist before his eyes. He knew that he was incapable of putting his thoughts into words—he was drunk, and therefore words had become dissociated from their meaning and bore no relation to those strange glimpses of truth that drunkenness induces.

"Listen to me. . . . It is true that I was promised . . . But . . ."

"Enough of that!"

Without warning, in a sudden burst of fury, Cosson swept all the bottles and glasses off the table.

"You make me sick! There! Satisfied? I had decided to kill myself on the grave the day of the funeral. I took a revolver with me. Because that, too, seemed a fine thing to do. Then I saw you. You didn't even notice that I was looking at you. Oh, no, not you. You just went on chatting with the other people at the funeral, most of whom were patients of yours. . . . Just like a Member of Parliament with his constituents."

It was perfectly true! Bergelon was struck by the simile. He had forgotten those personal exchanges in the cemetery. But now, suddenly, he recalled that Halkin the blacksmith, among others, had spoken to him—saying that he was having trouble with his liver—and that he had prescribed a suitable remedy!

"I tried going back home and returning to the bank. . . . But the people at the bank disgusted me as much as you do. . . . Give me a drink, Cécile."

"There's none left."

"Go and get a bottle from the bistro."

She went out, still wearing her housecoat.

Scarcely had she left the room than Cosson shouted:

"Do you see that? Now there's a girl! You examine her every week, so you know her as well as I do. But that doesn't prevent her from being worth more than all of you. . . . I always knew that. . . . I knew it even when I was still with my wife. . . . What, do you think, was the first thing my wife made me do? Eh? Guess!"

He slumped down on the edge of the bed next to the doctor, then laid a hand on his knee.

"She made me take out a life insurance policy. And I

did. I would have done anything. Because I wanted, at whatever cost . . . Do you understand? I'm the son of a humble village policeman. . . ."

He was crying, crying like a child now, with his face buried in his hands.

He was dead drunk. His speech was very slurred.

"She's gone to get some liquor. . . . You see . . . And all of you . . . You sent a policeman to question the neighbors. . . ."

"I swear to you . . ."

His drunkenness was reaching its climax.

"Don't swear . . . it won't do any good. . . . I said I was going to kill you, and I will. . . . I don't know when, as yet. . . . But sooner or later, when I've had as much as I can take . . . You don't understand that either, do you?"

His hand was still on Bergelon's knee, and Bergelon was filled with a longing to talk, to have his say, to break out of this stifling cocoon in which he felt himself imprisoned.

"I knew . . ." he said, speaking with difficulty and holding up a finger, like a man about to make an important pronouncement.

"What?"

"Everything! I, too, am a man who . . . For a start, my father was a drunkard."

"What's that got to do with it?"

"It's the same thing as having a village policeman for a father."

That was not what he had intended to say, but he knew what he meant.

"And when he died, my mother couldn't wait to get away and go to live in the country. . . . In Poitiers, I had a mistress who . . ."

He frowned. It was all so clear in his mind, a chain of

events, all linked together. But when he tried to put his thoughts into words, they no longer made sense.

"You see, my dear fellow . . ."

"You're unhappy, do you mean?"

"It's not that. . . ."

His throat felt raw from the red wine. He was afraid he was going to be sick.

"There are some things that I am capable of understanding, because I . . . I . . . you can see . . . I . . ."

"Are you afraid I'm going to kill you?"

"No."

"Well! I swore that I would. . . . Never mind! Even if, now . . ."

The table was swaying. The bed was heaving, up to the ceiling, down to the floor, like an elevator, and all the while the sewing machine purred on.

"You can do what you like, but you must understand . . . about Mandalin, for one thing. . . . Well, you see . . ."

What had he been going to say? Then another random thought came into his head:

"And the inspector, earlier on . . . I showed that inspector the door. . . ."

Which was not quite true, but nevertheless, that was what he had wanted to do.

"As for Cécile, even if she was ill, I . . ."

Footsteps on the stairs. Cosson tried to stand up, but he fell back onto the bed.

"Maybe it's true, all you're saying. But having once sworn . . ."

She came in, almost smiling—serene, at any rate— carrying a bottle of vermouth.

"This is all I could find."

She took a corkscrew from a drawer.

"Shh!" hissed Cosson. "There's no point in frightening him. Sooner or later I will kill him, but . . ."

". . . that's no reason to . ." said Bergelon, helping him out.

". . . that's no reason . . . Look here . . . Take a soldier's life, for instance . . ."

This time he did succeed in standing up, but the effort sent him sprawling across the table, almost tipping it over. She caught him as he fell, and he held on to her.

"Pour us a drink, Cécile."

Bergelon had closed his eyes for a moment, when the sound of a popping cork made him start.

"Sooner or later, I will kill him, but meanwhile give him a drink."

Her sky-blue housecoat brushed against him. He caught a faint whiff of light scent and felt the touch of a hand.

"Would you rather not?"

"I insist."

He rose to his feet. He was being held by the scruff of his neck. The sickly taste of vermouth in his mouth and throat; then blobs of light, two, three, five, ten, almost circular like halos, in the dimness of the room.

A woman's voice, far, very far, away, spoke:

"You'd better lie down as well, Jean."

And then someone laughed.

"All the same, I'll have to kill him, won't I? I know what I'll do. . . . I'm not in the least sleepy. . . . I'm going to the cemetery. . . ."

Confused noises . . . The mattress sagged. . . . An elbow dug into his ribs. . . .

Chapter Five

He knew all about it. Lying in a tangle of damp sheets, he opened one eye, small, round, black, and cold, and focused it unwaveringly on Germaine. He felt no surprise, no sense of transition from sleep to wakefulness.

She had been crying. It was late, ten o'clock at least, since more than half the bedroom was in full sunlight. And Bergelon, lying motionless, was in an evil mood and knew it.

There was no need for him to make an effort. Everything that had happened yesterday and today was perfectly clear in his mind: the people, the words, the feelings. He could also see Germaine only too clearly, not that she was to blame for that. It was simply that this morning, as far as he was concerned, everything was too clearly in focus, too sharply defined.

She had been crying. So what? There was nothing especially admirable in that, particularly as she had made no effort to conceal the fact; she was parading her reddened eyelids in a reproachful manner.

Why was it that, in a sudden flash, he could see her as a widow? He saw her in her widow's weeds, entangled in yards of black veiling, her eyes redder than ever, her mawkish sweetness even more pronounced, gazing sorrowfully about her, as widows do.

"What is it?"

He had spoken, still lying on his side, looking at her with that single eye, the other being buried in the pillow.

"This has come for you."

She must have been standing there in the bedroom for some time, watching him, waiting for him to wake up. With an exaggerated air of concern she laid an envelope on the bed beside him, and he saw that the writing was Cosson's.

"Aren't you going to read it? Do you know who it's from?"

So she knew. Oh, yes, she knew all right. He picked it up, stuffed the other pillow—his wife's—behind his back, and sat up.

"What are you waiting for?" he grumbled, knowing full well that she was determined to stay.

"I want to know what he's written. He came here this morning."

He looked up, interested.

"The children had left for school. I'd left the door unlocked for the grocer while I was rinsing my wash in the yard. When I heard someone moving around in the entrance hall I thought it must be the grocer. I was just wringing out the pillowcases when suddenly the back door burst open, and I saw him standing there, wearing no hat or tie. He said:

" 'Don't let me disturb you. . . . I presume your husband is still asleep? I'd be obliged if you would give him this. Tell him I'll come by to pick up my hat another time. . . .' "

Germaine bent down and took from a chair a gray felt hat unlike any that Bergelon had ever possessed. It was too big for him and very dirty. Germaine's lips were trembling, as if she was about to burst into tears again.

"What does he say in his letter?"

Why had she not begun by referring to the manner in which Bergelon had come home? That was the one thing he could not remember. He had a vague recollection of falling down the stairs at Cosson's place—or, rather, Cécile's—and of hearing the shoemaker grumbling behind his door. It had been raining. A sudden storm, no doubt. Certainly there was a freshness and a sparkle in the air this morning, such as usually follows a storm, and he could see streaks of moisture on all the roofs across the way.

"Did I manage the stairs on my own?" he asked, feeling neither shame nor remorse.

"I had already been out three times to look for you. Emile was crying, and I couldn't get him off to sleep. It was just after the storm broke. There was a flash of lightning, and it was then that I saw a sort of shadowy outline on the sidewalk. . . ."

He smiled. Just because, for the first time, she had scooped him, dead drunk, up from the sidewalk, she was well on the way to seeing herself as a martyr, if not a saint.

All the same, he did feel a little ashamed of himself, though not on that account. He was ashamed of his callous detachment and spontaneous cruelty. For so many years now they had lived together and shared the same bed. Together they had produced two children and had spent hours, day after day, night after night, watching over them in their beds. And yet, in spite of all that, he suddenly found himself looking at her as if she were a total stranger.

"Did you carry me up to bed?"

"I made you drink some coffee   . I got you onto your feet. . . . Annie saw you. . . ."

She turned her head away and stared at the floor, which glittered like a galaxy with little dancing specks of sunlight.

"Read it," she begged.

He tore open the envelope.

What if I should toss a bomb into your house? The notion occurred to me just this morning. I realize that the use of bombs has gone out of fashion. All the same, on reflection, it's not such a bad idea. And there are clear instructions for making them in my chemistry textbook. It's very simple.

Which doesn't necessarily mean that that is what I will do.

This part of the letter was written in violet ink, with the last sentence underlined.

Some time had apparently elapsed before Cosson had resumed:

I keep thinking of all sorts of things that it didn't occur to me to say to you last night. But Cécile complains that I am preventing her from getting any sleep. For my part, I have been awake since five this morning, and I don't even have a hangover.

I have promised myself that after I have delivered this letter to you by hand I will spend the rest of the day in bed asleep. Isn't it crazy? Nowadays I am free to go to sleep whenever I feel like it.

Bergelon put the letter down on the bedside table; with a sigh, he got out of bed and hunted for his slippers.

"Will you not allow me to read it?"

He stood looking at her for a long time. Oh, well, on her own head be it! He shrugged his shoulders and, with a sigh, said before going into the bathroom:

"If you insist!"

He turned on the shower. Seeing his wife waiting for him in the doorway, he deliberately prolonged the pleasurable sensation of water cascading over his body.

"Why don't you report him to the police?"

"Because there's nothing they can do to help."

"They could arrest him."

"The worst he'd get would be two weeks in jail for threatening behavior, and even then it would probably be a suspended sentence. . . . And then what?"

"Elie!"

He was lathering his face with shaving soap and gazing at his reflection in the mirror.

"This is what you must do. . . . Write to your substitute immediately. Instead of going on vacation next month as arranged, we'll go now, at once. . . ."

It affected him strangely to realize how remote she was from him. She would insist on interfering, on getting in on the act; the more she persisted, the wider the gulf between them.

"Any phone messages?" he asked, in his normal, everyday voice.

"One, from Madame Portal. You're not feeling too tired? Don't you feel ill?"

"Not in the least."

He dried his face and dabbed a little talcum powder on his cheeks.

"Elie!"

If she bleated out his name in that whining tone five hundred thousand times, it would make no difference. She felt she was being towed along in his wake. She was doing her best to hold on. What was there for her to hold on to, for God's sake?

By now he had resumed his everyday appearance and was moving with exaggerated steadiness.

"Are you looking for your hat? I'll get you the blue one."

And she had to stand on tiptoe and stretch up to the top shelf of the wardrobe to reach it.

"Are you going to see Madame Portal?"

"I am. If anyone phones, tell them I'll be back about one, as usual."

As he was leaving he was about to kiss her on the forehead, as one tosses a coin to a beggar, but she seemed to him so inept, so boring in her distress, that he could not bring himself to do so. She would, in fact, have made an exemplary widow, of the sort so well respected in provincial towns. As he went downstairs it occurred to him that there were a great many widows in their own town, indeed on Rue Pasteur alone. It had never struck him before. Were there really more widows than widowers, or was it that women paraded their widowhood because they saw it as a kind of rebirth?

He went into his consulting room, merely to pick up his bag of instruments, and decided to do his rounds on foot. What a strange document that letter of Cosson's was, especially the latter part! It was also strange that it should have been delivered so early in the morning. . . . And the way he had sneaked into the house, as if to see . . . to breathe in the atmosphere.

Preposterous as it might seem, his behavior was almost like that of a man in love. He had written:

I keep thinking of all sorts of things that it didn't occur to me to say to you last night.

But he would get around to saying them eventually! There would be more letters to follow, Bergelon had no doubt about that. Maybe this very night . . .

He felt just the least little bit lightheaded, rather a pleasant sensation, especially out here in the quiet sunlit streets, streaked with shadows and humming with distant sounds.

Madame Portal was the wife of Oscar Portal, owner of the brewery on Rue des Bourges. For months now Bergelon had been going by to see her every morning, and if he did not arrive by nine o'clock she would have him summoned peremptorily by telephone.

There was perhaps no house that gave him greater pleasure to visit. Above all he loved the yard, crowded with drays and horses, with casks being rolled about and straw everywhere. It seemed ablaze in the sunshine, and there were muscular men in blue, heaving heavy loads.

The smell of the yard permeated the whole house—a unique smell, a blend of beer, the urine of horses, and yeast. A small glass cubicle served as an office, but when Portal was not out on his rounds, he spent most of his time in the yard; he was a tall, ruddy, heavily built man, full of vigor, like his horses, his glowing complexion enhanced by a silver mustache that was turned up at the ends with a curling iron.

"Hello, doctor. On your way up?"

On his way out the doctor was always met with the same bold, frank, questioning look.

"Well?"

The answer never varied. For more than a year now,

Madame Portal had been confined to her bedroom upstairs, her swollen legs immersed in an enamel basin.

Whenever Portal referred to her disability, he would
say:

"She's waterlogged. She swells up, and then the swelling goes down, but it's always water."

There was the same smell on the stairs as in the yard.
The walls were papered with colored posters advertising
Portal beers and the firm's tonic water, manufactured
under the trade name Eau Cristal.

Bergelon knew that as soon as she heard his step on
the stairs the cook would be drawing him a well-chilled
glass of beer, ready for him to drink on his way out.

"Do sit down, doctor."

Madame Portal was a fine-looking woman. At least
she had been. Her face had not lost its beauty, especially
in the soft light that filtered through the drawn curtains,
which she would occasionally reach out to pull back a
little. Across her knees lay a dressmaker's tape measure;
every hour on the hour the poor soul would measure the
circumference of her legs.

"I've lost another half centimeter, doctor. . . . Tell me
. . . my son will be here on vacation in September this
year. Do you think that by then I might be fit to get up?"

She would never again leave her bed. It was miracle
enough that she had stayed alive so long.

"I don't see why not . . . if you take proper care and
don't allow yourself to get upset."

As she lay there in her bedroom she was forever strain-
ing to hear every sound in the house, striving to interpret
its significance.

"If you only knew what it was like being shut up in
here day in and day out! Sometimes when I want something, it's half an hour before anyone comes. . . ."

Why had they not thought of installing an electric bell

for her? Whatever the reason, her only means of summoning help was by banging on the floor with a walking stick.

"At this time of year my husband is never at home. Sometimes he's away for three whole days at a time. I can't help wondering what the children are up to in the meantime."

As far as her daughter was concerned, Bergelon could have told her. Her name was Eveline. She was just a little over fifteen, with a well-developed figure. He had examined her at the end of last winter because her mother feared that she was anemic. More than once he had seen her after dark, lurking on the porch of the house, and she had not been alone. The doctor had seen her with three different boys at least, and on one occasion he had recognized a married man who lived in the neighborhood.

"May I consult you on a rather delicate matter, doctor?"

She was always consulting him about something or other. She was up to all kinds of tricks to prolong his visits. When he stood up, she always looked so crestfallen that he often felt obliged to sit down again for a few more minutes.

"Is it possible for a man . . . a healthy man . . . a man of some considerable strength . . . Would it be possible for such a man to go for months without having . . . relations?"

But for the waxen pallor of her face, she would have blushed.

Her face was so expressive of genuine shyness that for an instant she looked twenty years younger.

"Please be frank with me. My husband claims that it is possible. . . . But I have been told so often that it isn't so! Everyone is so anxious to spare me distress. . . ."

She was on the verge of tears. She, who by rights

should have been dead long ago, was almost in tears at the thought that her stallion of a husband might have a mistress or two!

"There's no reason at all . . ." stammered Bergelon.

"What do you mean? No reason why he shouldn't?"

"Of course not! There's no reason why a man shouldn't wait."

"I'm just being silly, aren't I?"

She almost succeeded in touching his heart. Briefly he saw her bathed in a romantic glow—and then there was a click in his head, as sudden and sharp as the closing of a camera shutter, just as there had been when he had awakened this morning. Now he could see her in sharp focus, as she really was. He saw the monstrously bloated legs in the enamel basin, the waxen skin, the straggling hair; he became aware of the stale odor of the sickroom.

"Come on, stop worrying. . . . I really must be off now."

"Listen, doctor. Please don't say anything about this to him. Promise me."

Downstairs, the kitchen door stood open.

"No change, I suppose?" murmured the cook, who had the beer ready for him. "How it does drag on!"

And she added:

"She has me running up and down the stairs all day long for no reason at all. 'What is Monsieur doing? Has he had a good lunch? What was he wearing when he went out? Has Mademoiselle Eveline been reading those books on the top shelf of the bookcase?' And then she's forever asking questions about Joséphine. . . ."

Joséphine was the little maid, rosy-cheeked, plump, and round-eyed.

"I think she's jealous of Joséphine. She's always asking me if she's making eyes at Monsieur, and suspects her of deliberately loitering in the yard and the office. . . ."

90

Bergelon smiled. He knew friend Portal well enough to be sure that Joséphine had not been in the house a week before he was after her.

As he crossed the yard he was met with the usual questioning glance.

"No change?"

"None."

"No change" in this house meant that the patient had not yet died. They were bursting at the seams with money. When the children were small they were the only ones in the district to own a cart, drawn first by a goat and later by a donkey. The boy, now fourteen and still at school, was bone idle. As for Eveline, Bergelon had no doubt that any day now she would be turning up at his office. . . .

Bergelon pulled himself up short. Something was stirring at the back of his mind, but it was still too vague and indistinct to be called an idea. Maybe he ought to drop by and pass the time of day with old Hautois. He, too, was dying, but his only worry was that the doctor might forget to bring him a present of snuff.

There was wash spread out to dry on the grass in the meadow. A woman was bending down to gather it up, and he could see her stocking tied above the knee with a piece of red string.

What more was there that Cosson wanted to say to him? Had he really seriously considered blowing up his house with dynamite?

He was seized with a sudden fit of anguish after his fourth visit, to a child with mumps who moaned that the room was filled with floating demons, swelling and shrinking alternately, and pressing down on his chest.

"You've been feeding him, haven't you?"

"Just eggs beaten up in milk and some dry crackers."

"That's too much. He should have nothing but plain milk."

He felt more than a little foolish to find that his fears had been groundless. His house was still standing in its proper place on the street. In the distance he could see his son on the way home from school, running his ruler along the walls of the houses to make it bounce between the stones.

The atmosphere at lunch was unpleasant, like discordant music. Germaine, in the role of brave little woman, held back her tears and put on a cheerful smile. She tried to bring the children into the conversation, for they must on no account be allowed to dwell on their father's ignominious return home the previous night.

"We'll see if we can get the same villa we had last year. Maybe, if it could be arranged, we could stay there an extra two weeks."

"I will sleep in my tent on the beach!" declared Emile, knowing full well that he would be allowed to do no such thing.

Bergelon, in spite of himself, behaved as if he was thoroughly ashamed. He dared not look his children in the eye—especially his daughter, who, in her turn, was careful to avoid speaking to him. For the first time it occurred to him that one day Annie, too, might lurk on the porch after dark with a boy, laughing shrilly every now and then, like Eveline Portal.

"Don't you agree, Father?"

He jumped. It was his wife who had spoken.

"What?"

"If we can't find anywhere to stay at Riva-Bella, we'll go to Lion-sur-Mer instead."

The names of these resorts evoked for him a totally different world: the little villas of Riva-Bella were like dolls' houses, built of cardboard and painted in bright colors; under a clear, blue sky, the vast golden beaches were dotted with half-naked people and beach umbrellas. Hour upon hour of nothingness, followed by a cold meal in the evening; the stove smelling of kerosene; the uncomfortably narrow beds; and the racket from a nearby dance hall going on until one o'clock in the morning, followed by a stream of boys and girls singing as they went past the house.

Germaine did not swim. She never even wore a bathing suit because she was reluctant to display her varicose veins. Emile adored the pinball machines. Sometimes Bergelon would spend a long time observing the antics of some pretty girl with a well-developed figure; then, seeing her dressed, he would blush to discover that she was only a kid, scarcely older than Annie.

"Don't you want any strawberries?"

What, when all was said and done, had she brought into his life? He was thinking of Germaine: he saw her again as she had looked at that fateful fair, in her white dress, her straw hat trimmed with blue ribbon, her swaying walk, her graceful fragility.

Graceful fragility, indeed! She had been in poor health, that was all. And that timid, disarming smile meant no more than that she was eager to be married. It was not inconceivable that from the age of ten she had already made up her mind to be his wife. What was so odd was that she had succeeded.

Once again he asked himself, What had she brought him? She had seen to it that their house was properly furnished and decorated, but all according to her own taste. And he suddenly realized that it was also according to her own taste that she had organized their life together.

She had just given proof of this by referring to Riva-Bella. He detested the place. What was there for him to do there? If he so much as set foot in the casino, she would sigh and murmur reproachfully:

"You will be careful, won't you, Elie?"

For—perish the thought—he might lose twenty or fifty francs at lotto! Since she did not dance, he could hardly take the floor with a stranger. Nor could he join the young people at play on the beach while she sat knitting under her umbrella.

He spent all his days reading or lounging with his eyes shut, seeing, as he had as a child, flickering images forming and dissolving against the luminous reddish background of his closed eyelids.

"Go and open up, Mimile."

It was time for his office. The door was unlatched, the electric buzzer turned on. He drank his coffee. He felt drowsy. Only now was he beginning to feel the effects of the exhausting night before. He experienced a faint sense of nausea.

It was not inconceivable that Cosson might return with a parcel under his arm, a bomb . . . or a revolver, perhaps. He went into the office, his lips twisted in a little crooked smile.

The buzzer! Someone had arrived . . . two people, he could see them through the glass, a mother and her daughter. The girl was thin, fifteen or sixteen years old. Another case of anemia . . . hemoglobin . . . an injection . . . fresh air and exercise . . . and off you go!

Throughout the afternoon he jumped every time the buzzer sounded, but there was no sign of Cosson, nor was any letter dropped into the mailbox.

Tea time . . . Germaine, all melancholy and resignation . . . He still had two or three more visits to make in the neighborhood. On his way he encountered a funeral procession of a somewhat modest kind and wondered who had died. . . . Not one of his patients, at any rate.

As he was turning the corner at the end of the street he almost bumped into someone.

"Excuse me, doctor."

It was Cécile, wearing her white hat and blue suit. Cécile, looking as she always did—tall, serene, with those amber eyes flecked with gold.

"I hope it doesn't embarrass you to be seen talking to me in the street."

"Not in the least."

"Have you a minute or two to spare? I could walk with you."

There was not a soul on the street, except for one person: that happened to be Madame Pholien, the worst gossip in the neighborhood.

"You saw the state Jean was in, didn't you?"

Could Madame Pholien possibly be imagining that the two of them were on their way to the hotel? Cécile, still in her quiet manner, asked:

"What do you make of it?"

What on earth did she mean?

"I think . . . What can I say? . . ."

They were going past the wall of the school he had attended as a child. In those days there lived just across the road a kept woman, a beautiful blonde with a luscious figure, who received visits two or three times a week from a judge. It was the talk of the town. She had had a child by him, a boy named Albert. For a long time Bergelon and Albert had been friends, and on one occasion Bergelon had been invited to the house; he had been much impressed by its plush elegance.

"I promise you, he's not out of his mind. I know him well, better than anyone else. He's very high strung, but he's genuine. . . ."

No doubt they were being spied on by people standing at their windows, but what the doctor found most embarrassing was that Cécile was taller than he.

"I've done everything possible to quiet him down. I know how to handle him. I tried to persuade him to leave the district. I was willing to go with him. But I failed, and for that reason I think it would be wiser if you were to go away."

Was it not astonishing that he did not even flinch?

"Does Cosson know you have come to see me?"

"No. I'll tell him when I get back. I only thought of it a little while ago, after I was already in town."

The words "in town" had a special significance in her vocabulary. They meant that she was out on the beat in search of some gentleman, preferably a middle-aged man.

"If you don't go away, I'm convinced he'll do something foolish. . . . What good would that do you? The vacation season has already begun. . . ."

Lowering her voice, she murmured, as if to herself:

"I know what I'm talking about!"

Then, returning to the attack:

"I presume that you will be going on vacation yourself? By the time you get back I'll have had time . . ."

She and Germaine were of one mind! Except that Germaine was bent on getting her husband away, whereas Cécile was endeavoring to persuade the other man to leave town.

"I don't know what you think of him. If you knew him as well as I do, you would realize that he's the salt of the earth. He's too good, too genuine, too generous. . . . I hope you don't mind my talking to you like this?"

The square, with its trees, its deserted benches, its green carriage gates leading to patrician mansions.

"I know he delivered a letter to you by hand this morning. He told me that there was nothing very wicked in it, that it was just a bit of fun. For the moment he's asleep. . . . Only I'm afraid . . ."

A car, long-bodied, black, and gleaming. Mandalin's. And Mandalin, with his rabbity profile, leaning forward to get a better view, acknowledging Bergelon's presence with a slight wave of the hand. And what must he be thinking? After all, didn't everyone know perfectly well that Madame Mandalin . . . ?

"Are you in a hurry? I'll be off, then. . . . The only way to avoid more serious trouble is to do as I ask. . . . He's obsessed with this notion of his that he's got to kill you. He's quite capable of doing it for no better reason than because he said he would."

Then, suddenly, taking the doctor by surprise:

"Good night, doctor."

Too late! She was gone. She had turned off onto a dark little side street, which abutted onto the back yards of a row of tall tenements.

He had not had time to . . . He had not had time for anything.

Not even to absorb the fact of her presence.

In a few minutes, some local farmer, some traveling salesman, it did not matter who, as long as he had fifty or a hundred francs in his pocket . . .

He walked on, visiting only one in three of the patients he ought to have seen. He felt cheated, on returning home, to find the mailbox empty. He was impelled to ask Germaine:

"Any callers?"

"Only the gas man."

"No letters?"

He knew that she understood, or rather he thought she did.

"None."

Chapter Six

He had been awake for some time, lying motionless, stark naked, on his bed, when there was a knock on the door. There was no trace of drowsiness in his voice as he called out:

"Who is it?"

He had not yet rung for his breakfast.

"Your mail, sir."

"Come in."

At that same moment another body, naked as his own, stirred beneath the sheets and scrambled across Bergelon.

"Not yet, you fool!"

The body that hurled itself across the room toward the bathroom had legs, thighs, arms, and shoulders tanned by the sun, but the buttocks were pale and the tangle of hair inky black.

"The door is locked!" protested the chambermaid, rattling the doorknob to no effect.

"I'm coming."

Still naked, he opened the door. The chambermaid, a woman of forty or fifty, looked at him disdainfully and handed him his letters. As soon as he had shut the door, his companion came back into the room, going toward the bed; this time it was her white belly that caught his eye.

"Did you do it on purpose?" she asked, referring to the fact that Bergelon had opened the door to the maid without putting on any clothes.

She was neither indignant nor surprised. Rather, she seemed amused. There was a flicker of mockery in her brown eyes, and the doctor was almost tempted to slip into his dressing gown. But never mind. It had been an odd thing to do! He was not going to allow her to humiliate him. And—still naked—he seated himself in a grubby velvet armchair, crossed his legs, and ignoring his reflection in the wardrobe mirror opposite, glanced at the three envelopes in his hand.

The woman had gotten back into bed and was lying curled up like a cat, with the sheet gathered around her like a sack bulging with the outline of her rump; her eyes glittered through the dark thicket of hair spread out on the pillow.

Before opening his letters Bergelon lit a cigarette. It was a mild, gray day. The sea, too, was gray and still, edged with a narrow ribbon of white all along the sand. It must have rained late the night before, for the beach was darker than usual, fawn rather than golden. People could be heard going down onto the sand, families with children, chattering and shrieking. The French windows opened onto a rustic-style balcony, fenced in by a blue wooden balustrade. The scene below was like a bazaar, with deck chairs and shrimping nets piled up all over the place.

Bergelon looked uncertainly from one to another of his three letters: one from his mother, who always wrote on black-edged note paper, one from his wife, and the last from Cosson.

He decided to keep Cosson's until the end, the better to savor it, and began by opening the one from his mother, whose hard, straight, angular handwriting was occasionally varied with unexpected loops.

My dear son,

I heard only yesterday from old Collard, who is now almost seventy-three (it was he who brought you home in his wheelbarrow that time when you fell from an apple tree and broke your leg. He's never forgotten it and refers to it every time we meet), that you are not in Bugle but have gone off on vacation by yourself. Old father Collard still goes to market every week to sell his butter and eggs. He wanted to consult you about his eyes, as his sight continues to deteriorate, in spite of all the spectacles prescribed for him. But he found only your substitute there.

You have often asked me to accompany you on vacation at the shore, and you have never understood why I always refuse. I have nothing against your wife, though I must say that she was not much of a catch for you. You could have aspired to anyone. I still think that she set her cap for you, and her mother likewise. Apropos of her mother, I hear that she has just sold that house of hers in Lagneux, which was the only property that Germaine could look forward to inheriting from her, for 60,000 francs. Her reason for doing so, apparently, was to come to the rescue of your wife's sister, who married some good-for-nothing who has just gone bankrupt yet again.

So, as you are on your own in Riva-Bella, I am willing to come and join you, provided that it is convenient to you and that it is understood that I have no wish to be a burden to anyone. You must, indeed, be thoroughly exhausted to have gone off on vacation before the rest of your family, and I cannot help wondering whether there isn't something else behind it. You will wear yourself out for people who don't pay their bills and who are not even grateful for what you do.

Hoping to hear from you soon,

Yours affectionately,

Mother

"Interesting news from home?" asked Edna, reaching for her cigarettes.

"It's from my mother."

Still sitting naked, with his legs crossed, he tore open his wife's letter.

My dear Elie,

The children have just left for school, and before getting down to preparing their lunch, I am writing these few lines to give you the latest news from home.

First, I must tell you about C——, whom I have seen several times in the street. He must have found out that you had gone away and that your work had been taken over by a substitute. For the first few days I feared for the children, and I took them to and from school, which wasn't easy, seeing that Annie's school is so far away from the boys' school. I must tell you that we have had a whole series of storms, one of them so heavy that the cellar was flooded. Luckily, Monsieur Charles was good enough to help me clear up the mess. I'll tell you more about that later. For the present we are having fine weather once more, although it is still very hot.

To return to C——, I have not seen him wandering in

this neighborhood for the past two days, and I must say it's a great relief. I always thought he would lose interest, given time, and that that sort of obsessional fixation couldn't last long. Anyway, I have warned everyone not to give him your address. But don't fail to send me a telegram immediately if he follows you to Riva-Bella.

On Sunday Monsieur Charles's mother came to see us. She's very well bred, very distinguished, and although she's only forty-eight, her hair is as white as snow. She's come all the way from the Jura especially to see her son. She brought toys for the children, though she must have forgotten to ask how old they were, as she brought a doll for Annie and a toy farm for Mimile. Well, after all, it's the thought that counts!

She's a woman who has suffered a great deal. Her husband was a flourishing timber merchant in the Vosges and then suddenly, without warning, he became infatuated with a singer whom he had met in the neighboring town, and he ran off with her. He's never been heard from since. No one even knows his whereabouts. To make matters worse, before leaving he drew every penny he possessed out of the bank, so there was no alternative but to sell the sawmill.

As for Monsieur Charles himself, he is far and away the pleasantest and best-mannered substitute you have ever had. I've heard him with my own ears tell some of your patients, the sort who are always trying to worm information out of you (like Madame Pholien, for instance!) that, having prescribed such and such treatment for them, you must have had your reasons, and that their best course was to carry on as before.

In the evening he plays his violin, and he plays very well. So much so that Annie has decided she would like to start taking music lessons next term. I pointed out that the piano was a more suitable instrument for a girl, but you know how stubborn she can be. Fortunately, it's a long time from now to the end of the school vacation!

Imagine my surprise when, on his third day here, I went upstairs to do his room and found that he had already done it himself. When I spoke to him about it he said that he could not think of letting me make his bed and empty his trash. He's certainly a very different type from the man who took over from you last year. Remember the mess he left all over the house, and how he never stopped complaining?

I wish you would write to me at greater length, not just postcards. Have you made inquiries about the villa? Will it be available for next month? Have they raised the rent, as they were threatening to do last year?

I can't think of anything else I ought to mention, except to implore you to rest as much as possible and to take things quietly for the sake of your nerves. The children will be writing to you this evening.

> Yours most affectionately,
> Germaine

He read it very slowly, in little sips, with a malicious glint in his eye. What emerged most clearly from the letter was a portrait of the face and figure of Monsieur Charles, as his wife called him—his surname was difficult to pronounce, Weschmuller or something of the sort. Monsieur Charles, whom he saw as a tall, blond young man, with closely cropped hair and dreamy eyes behind thick spectacles with gold frames. Worthy Monsieur Charles! Germaine had lost no time in taking him to her heart. It was as if overnight he had completely taken over from Bergelon.

And that tale about the father who had run off with a singer, without a word of warning.

"Why are you smiling?"

"No reason . . . I'm just smiling. . . ."

"Is she still refusing you a divorce?"

Ah, yes, he had almost forgotten that he had told her he was in the process of seeking a divorce. He had not meant it to be taken seriously. Anyway, it was she who had first raised the question.

Besides, his affair with Edna (somehow he could not get used to the name) meant nothing. It was totally unrelated to what had gone before and to what might happen in the future. It was just something he had stumbled into by accident.

On his first day at the Hôtel Bellevue, where he was staying, she had caught his attention because she was wearing the scantiest of sundresses, and her firm, well-proportioned little body was very brown. She was wearing pink polish on her fingernails and toenails, and had heavy bracelets on her wrists. Her eyes were as dark as her hair.

She was known as "the lady with the little boy," because she had a son. He was a kid of eight or nine, an amazingly beautiful child, dark-haired like his mother, but with huge, clear blue eyes fringed with dark lashes, which made him look like a girl.

What most impressed the other hotel guests was the boy's self-possession. His manners were already those of an adult. He made no demands whatsoever on his mother, and he replied to all questions with exquisite politeness.

Bergelon had not yet grown accustomed to being on his own. He had taken no active steps in the matter. He had strolled along the beach, telling himself that he was free to do as he pleased, but having no idea how to go about it. The previous year, for instance, the thought had often crossed his mind that, but for the presence of his wife, he could have . . .

Could have done what, exactly? Most of the people

there were with their families or friends. He roamed around, surrounded by young girls, with an uneasy feeling that he was behaving a bit like a dirty old man. Quite by chance, he had sat down not far from the lady with the little boy, who, covered in suntan oil and naked but for a scanty scrap of gaudily striped material, used to lie motionless, basking in the sun for hours on end. He had spoken to her, offering her a cigarette, or something equally commonplace:

"Are you here on your own?"

"For the present I'm on my own here with my son."

He had accompanied her back to the hotel, carrying her deck chair. In view of her dark complexion, he had asked her if she was a foreigner. She, not very originally, asked him to guess.

In the end, it turned out that she was Tunisian.

Or rather that it was in Tunis that she had met and married a distinguished settler? Was she or was she not divorced? Had she, in actual fact, ever been married?

He did not greatly care. His only regret was that he himself was not wholly unencumbered.

"I needn't ask you if you are married. I can see that you are wearing a wedding ring. Is your wife in Paris? Will she be joining you later?"

"It's not very likely," he replied, responding with a smile to her unspoken thoughts.

"Are you separated?"

"More or less."

"Getting a divorce?"

"You could say so."

"It's always so complicated!" she said, speaking as one who knew what she was talking about. "It can sometimes drag on for years, and difficulties often arise when least expected. How do you come to be called Elie, since you are obviously not Jewish?"

"Are you Jewish?"

"Isn't it obvious? I'm a Russian Jew, though I was born in Constantinople."

It made no difference to him. Constantinople . . . Tunis . . . As far as he was concerned, they were both no more than inlets on the map, bluer than the rest, surrounded by dazzlingly white ports, as illustrated on travel posters.

"I knew another French doctor, in Bizerte, a ship's surgeon who was a close friend of mine for some years. His name was Martin Chaffrier."

He started in surprise.

"Chaffrier? Tall and dark, with a scar on one cheek?"

"Do you know him?"

He was the man who, when they were both medical students in Poitiers, had shared a mistress with him. Elise! Elise Noireaud, so long buried in his memory, rising to the surface again like this!

"I think I've got a photograph of him somewhere in my bag."

And there, indeed, he was! Weatherbeaten now, more virile-looking than in the old days, mounted on a camel on some sightseeing trip.

"Whatever put it into your parents' head to call you Elie?"

"It was an obsession of my grandmother's. My mother's name was Judith, and one of my uncles was named Daniel."

Good heavens! He just remembered something else, going back even further than his shared love affair with Elise.

"My mother's grandmother . . . yes . . . that's right! My mother's grandmother, who married a miller near Bugle, her maiden name was Kridelka. . . ."

"That doesn't sound particularly Jewish."

"I thought it was an Eastern name, Armenian perhaps?"

She considered the matter, she for whom the world was more than a lot of patches of color on a map.

"It sounds more Hungarian," she said. "Or it might be Czech. . . . I've seen names like that on storefronts in Prague. . . . Kridelka . . . how very odd!"

Odder still was the way . . . That evening they had strolled together from one end of the beach to the other. They returned together to the Hôtel Bellevue. At the door of Edna's room, Bergelon murmured, as if he did not care one way or the other:

"Are you inviting me in?"

She put her finger to her lips and pointed to the adjoining door, behind which her son lay asleep.

"What about it?" he had whispered.

"What's the number of your room?"

"Twelve."

"Leave your door unlocked. Turn off the light."

A quarter of an hour later she had tiptoed into his room, in her dressing gown, smelling strongly of suntan lotion.

"Not in bed yet?"

Three nights had already passed since then!

But this was not his idea of love. She was too passionate, too ingenious, too full of tricks, claiming that he was totally inexperienced; she was bent on instructing him, always taking the initiative.

"I'd better go and get dressed!" she said forcefully, leaping out of bed in a single bound just as he was opening his third letter.

"Will you be coming to the beach this morning?"

"Yes . . . yes . . ." he replied absent-mindedly, while she put on her dressing gown and went out into the corridor. It was ten o'clock; by now everyone was up and about, which meant that their liaison must be the talk of the whole place.

It meant nothing at all. . . . A chance encounter . . . a passing fancy . . .

He glanced at his reflection in the mirror and took his dressing gown down from the hook. Then he rang for his breakfast and went out onto the balcony, which was wreathed in the same transparent mist as enveloped the rest of the town.

There were already people in the water. Others, dressed in black, thronged the streets, having just arrived by the local train. It took him a minute or two to realize that today was Sunday and that these people were visitors from the surrounding countryside.

Just about now Annie would be on her way to High Mass, with her white gloves and her missal. . . . Emile would be at a Scout meeting. . . . He wondered what Monsieur Charles did with his time on Sundays.

The chambermaid, scowling, slammed his breakfast tray down on the little bamboo table.

"When can I get in to do the room? I go off duty at noon on Sundays."

It did not matter to him. The letter . . . Cosson's letter . . .

I have managed it at last! Who could imagine that a problem that seemed so simple should turn out to be so hard to solve? I thought I would be able to get your address with no trouble at all. I knew from Cécile that you were going away, as she told me all about her meeting with you. She's a dear, good girl, but she doesn't understand. Now because she sees that I'm writing to you, she's inclined to believe that you are no longer in danger.

But before I say another word, I must warn you that nothing has changed. I don't know yet exactly when I shall be leaving for Riva-Bella, but you can expect me to turn up there any day now.

For the first few days I hung about near your house at the time when the postman delivers. I was hoping to slip inside and empty the mailbox, where I felt sure I should find a postcard from you. But your wife must have guessed what was in my mind, for she never once left the door on the latch.

Next I considered making an appointment with your substitute and spinning him a yarn about how it was absolutely essential that I get in touch with you personally by letter. But when he passed me one time in the street, I could tell by the way he looked at me that your wife had told him the whole story and that he was on his guard against me. For a moment I even thought he was going to speak to me. That was the last thing I wanted, because in spite of his meek and mild appearance, he's the sort who might easily give you a sock on the jaw when you least expect it, and besides, he's stronger than I am. You see, I make no pretense of being braver than I am!

It occurred to me that one of the children might be sent out to mail a letter to you. In that case I would have snatched it out of their hands, but that didn't happen either.

Cécile could see that I was getting into a state over it. She said that if I promised to behave myself, she would get me your address. And so she did. She simply stood on the corner of your street and waited for the postman. I don't know what she said to him, but the upshot is that he gave her your address.

I have so many things I want to say to you, but I don't know yet whether I shall be able to get them all down on paper.

Cécile thought that she had found a way of solving the whole problem. She wanted us to go off together to Morocco. She says that in a place like that, with so many army officers . . . It's not that I'm squeamish . . . feeling as I do now, I don't give a damn about anything. . . . All the same, if I were to go with her to Morocco, I'd be nothing better than a pimp.

I wonder if you are capable of understanding me? Sooner or later I will have to make up my mind to take action. You know what I mean. It's the only way to put an end to this thing once and for all. I won't attempt to escape. So much the worse for you! And I will forbid my lawyer to plead diminished responsibility, because I am perfectly sane.

You might as well admit it, because you know it's true! You and I are out of the same stable. Not like your friend, that imbecile Mandalin, who is a coward to boot! You know as well as anyone that I'm a decent man, one who believes everything he is told and who is easily led by the nose. Now, just suppose that what happened to me had happened to you. I was thinking about that only yesterday, watching your daughter on her way to school, full of airs and graces, very much the little lady.

Suppose that all of a sudden . . . And by foul play, do you see? By worse than foul play! You were aware of it yourself. You couldn't look me in the eye. You couldn't even bring yourself to lie to me. And at the funeral . . . Don't think I didn't have my eye on you!

You knew it was your fault that my wife was dead, that my child was dead. And all because Mandalin had promised you a fat fee.

Did you really imagine that I should just carry on as if nothing had happened, that I shouldn't understand? And to think that there are still hundreds of thousands, millions, of people as gullible as I was!

And what about the bank manager? When he heard that I'd started drinking, he sent one of the other cashiers, a half-witted old fool, to spy on me. The very day I stopped going to work he ordered a thorough investigation into my accounts. He imagined, poor idiot, that I must have been fiddling with the books!

And what do you suggest I do now? I certainly can't start again where I left off! Then what? Go to the cemetery with my arms full of flowers, maybe? Even though I know perfectly well that I myself meant nothing to Marthe? All she wanted was to be married, with a home of her own and children, and to be visited by her mother on Thursdays and, in company with her sister and brother-in-law, to return the visit on Sundays.

I'm sure you will do me the justice of admitting that I am not rushing things. I'm in no hurry. It seems I'm drinking too much. Even Cécile, though she doesn't say anything, tries to make me realize . . . Do you know how she's spending her time while I'm writing to you? She's sitting at the opposite end of the table, also writing a letter. From time to time our pens knock against each other as we dip into the inkwell. She is writing to her lover who is in Poissy. She always manages, somehow, to send him a little money. Next week, she will be going to visit him. She has asked me to go with her, not actually into the prison visiting room, but as far as Poissy, which would enable us to spend a few hours in Paris on the way back.

I haven't made up my mind yet. It all depends. . . . Maybe before then I will have decided to go to Riva-Bella. . . .

I had considered joining the Foreign Legion, but if the films I've seen are anything to go by, it's a pretty disgusting life, if all there is to it is harboring black thoughts and getting drunk in dubious nightclubs in the company of torch singers. . . .

From time to time I run into old friends in the street, in particular my former colleagues at the bank, and they cut me dead. The police are keeping an eye on me as well. Someone must have told them that I was liable to do someone harm.

Cécile is looking up at me, wanting to know how many *m*'s there are in *emmerder*. I haven't asked to see her letter, nor has she asked to see mine. All I know is that her father was a railroad signalman somewhere near Bourges, and that one of her brothers is a policeman. That's a laugh!

When I'm fed up with it here, I will take the train. . . . Maybe you and I will get drunk together just once more before I kill you. I've got a revolver. It belongs to that fellow who's doing time in Poissy. Cécile sewed it into the bolster. She knows I've got it, but all she said when she found out was, "You'll come to terms with things in the end, you'll see!" She was a bit worried, not knowing who would take your place at the weekly checkup. Apparently, he's an old fellow with a beard, who spends his whole time spouting obscenities. . . .

Bergelon smiled at this description of Mouvaux, from Saint-Eloi, a former army doctor who reminded him a little of his father, with the difference that Bergelon senior's vice had been drink, whereas Mouvaux's was women. In every other respect they were equally run-down and seedy. The lives of such men revolve around a single obsession, and outside that they have no interest in anything whatsoever!

A voice rose up to him from beneath the balcony.

"What is your charge for lunch?"

"Sixteen francs for a four-course meal of hors d'oeuvres, fish, meat, and dessert. That's without wine."

Bergelon leaned over the balcony. There was a man with his wife and three little tots behind him, armed with buckets and spades. He and his wife exchanged uneasy glances.

"How much for just one dish?"

"We only do a set lunch."

"Is it full price for children as well?"

The woman, in a flowered print dress, urged:

"Come on, Germain. . . ."

For she had just spotted a place opposite, offering a tourist menu at twelve francs.

It was going to rain again. All the gray moisture in the air was beginning to condense into a fine drizzle, depressing as a widow's weeds. The children could not play on the sand. The flowered print dress would be ruined. They must have been up very early in the morning, elbowing their way along some crowded station platform to get seats in a third-class railroad car.

The awning was being hastily lowered over the terrace of the hotel, where the tables were already laid, each one with its dish of radishes, shrimp, and beets.

"Hello."

It was Edna—he would never get used to that name, which so closely resembled that of the volcano—Edna who, wearing an overskirt and carrying a novel, her neat little bottom swaying from side to side, was making for the beach, where her son, all on his own, was building a sand castle.

"Hello," he replied without enthusiasm. Where was he in his letter?

She was a bit worried . . .

He had already read that.

. . . spouting obscenities . . .

That was it, he had got as far as "obscenities." It was odd to reflect that a little creature as ladylike as Edna, with a growing son of her own, could behave obscenely in their intimate relations. It was this, in fact, that most repelled Bergelon about her. Not to mention the fact that

she was wont to accompany her actions with a stream of
filthy language.

... obscenities ...

Cosson must have been drinking steadily as he wrote.
His handwriting, clear and neat at the beginning, was
growing larger and clumsier, with splashes of ink, as the
letter progressed:

They make me sick, all of them. I'll have to do something.
And you'll never guess what it is that will probably make up
my mind for me in the end. That's another of those hu-
miliating little secrets, that I won't confide even to Cécile.

It's that I have never seen the sea!

When they sent me away on vacation, it was always to
stay with an aunt in the suburbs of Bugle, whose house
overlooked the gasworks. This aunt took advantage of me
by making me work in her garden. And when I was called
up for my military service, I was posted to Lyons!

Later I never earned enough to be able to afford a
vacation. Marthe and I used to say that when her confinement had been paid for we would start saving up for a
month's vacation at the shore with the baby.

Now it is you who are at the shore. I don't know what
you have done to Cécile, but she certainly has a soft spot
for you. She assures me that, though you have gone away,
it is not because you are frightened, but because you want
to give me time to calm down.

In other words, to give me time to return to my job in
the bank, to work hours of overtime wearing a green eye-
shade because of those filthy electric light bulbs of theirs
which destroy your sight!

Cécile has already finished her letter. She'll be going out
in a minute. It's her time. I'm used to it. I'm not jealous.
On the contrary, it gives me great satisfaction to think that

a lot of oafs and pigs ... When she comes in, I make her tell me all about it in detail, and you can take my word for it, it's all highly edifying! If I felt like it, I could have a lot of fun telling the truth about some of those people!

It is my firm intention shortly to go and find out about the train schedules. I know already that the most convenient route is via Paris.

The shoemaker downstairs no longer even says good morning to me. The other day he announced to Cécile that the terms of her tenancy allowed for only one occupant, not two. But he never objected to her receiving as many as four or five clients in a single afternoon! And him with a fourteen-year-old daughter, who's forever loitering on the stairs!

It seems that there's a move afoot to sell off my furniture, because there's four months' rent owing on my apartment. I don't give a damn. The pork butcher can whistle for his rent!

What I am most anxious for you to know is that my plans are absolutely unchanged. When I'm really at the end of my tether I shall do what remains to be done. I think I'll drop the idea of a bomb. All the same, it would have been fun! But seeing that you yourself are away from home ...

I'm sure there are a lot more things I was meaning to say to you, but I can't remember what they are! I'm going to sleep now. I'm sick of all that riffraff at the Zanzi-Bar. They're all alike! My mother goes to church twice a day to pray for me. Which reminds me of the days when she used to make me go to Communion with her every morning, all through the month of May, which meant getting up at half past six, and all because she wanted me to help her carry the early gooseberries and cherries that we used to buy on the way back.

I have a feeling that it won't be long now before I take

that train. It's an intolerable situation. It's time I put an end to it.

So much the worse for you!

The signature was an illegible scrawl. Bergelon had a feeling that Cosson could not bear to bring his letter to an end, and that he would add innumerable postscripts.

In fact there was only one:

P. S. At any rate, before I come to see you, I will certainly treat myself to the luxury of a dip in the sea!

Chapter Seven

H*ave* you ever wished you could be someone other than yourself?"

Lying stretched out on her stomach, propped up on her elbows, she stared down at the sand. Although her face was so close to his, her voice sounded strange and distant in his ears, as though they were separated by a veil. She reminded him of a friend of his youth, who spoke in that same remote, indolent manner as he lay in bed, drugged with cocaine.

She looked up, glancing mechanically at her bronzed body, gleaming with oil.

"Why? Don't you like me as I am?"

He was secretly amused because, unknown to her, he was playing a game—a game of his own invention, or so he believed—which as a small boy he had called "shutters." Leaning well back in his deck chair, with the brim of his straw hat pulled down over his eyes, he would peer through a slit in his lids, as through a slatted shutter, and it was sometimes an effort to control the width of the slit. Thus, when Edna—he simply could not get used to that name!—when Edna had stirred at the sound of his voice, the shutters, as it were, had sprung wide apart. And so it was that she appeared to him merely as a figure in the foreground of a vast painting, dwarfed by great splashes of color, representing the sea, the sky, and the sand. To tell the truth, she was no more than a pale-green stain on the sand, for she was wearing a pale-green bathing suit; right next to her was another stain, the color of pink icing, outlining the figure of a fat young girl.

But even before she had opened her mouth to reply, he had lowered the shutters to a crack, so that she now loomed over him in close-up, with her face and figure sharply outlined, and he was able to observe the rather silly air of surprise—a commonplace manifestation of flirtatiousness—which his question had provoked, and the even sillier smile of mingled complacency and anxiety with which she contemplated her body:

"Don't you like me as I am?"

He reduced the slit further, bringing the details of her body into still sharper focus: the golden down on her upper lip, a birthmark the size of a ten-franc piece on her left shoulder blade, and just below the two curves of her buttocks, where the bathing suit was too tight, a few coarse, very black, curly hairs.

He could have answered:

"I wasn't thinking of you."

But why bother? She was not involved in the game he was playing. Her fingers, with their overlong, polished nails, were moving again, tracing heaven knows what symbols in the sand.

It was odd that the thought of cocaine should have come into his head, for it really was cocaine that had started him off on the game of shutters. Not that Bergelon had administered it to himself, of course. It had happened long ago, when he was still only a kid; it was then that he had invented the game.

He had been suffering from a toothache, and he had been given a tablet that must have contained a minute quantity of cocaine, just sufficient to leave an unfamiliar aftertaste in his mouth. He had been sitting under a fig tree. To protect his cheeks from the slightest draft, he had covered his face with a floral scarf, and he had remained there with his eyes half closed, then closed, then three-quarters open, allowing a series of fantastic images to drift across his vision. Now that he came to think of it, it had been the happiest experience of his life. It was also associated with his most tender memory of his mother, for just at that moment she had brought him out a glass of lemonade.

Here and now, things were a good deal more complicated, for the canvas was vast and filled with many and varied shapes and colors, and he had no scarf over his face. It was further complicated by the fact that he was playing the game not only in space but in time.

For instance, a few minutes ago he had focused on a patch of very pale, clear blue sea, divided from the sky—otherwise indistinguishable in color—by a ribbon of light. Floating in this golden zone, in total isolation, was a solitary boat.

Then merely by moving his eyelids, he had brought into being a human figure, standing upright, dressed in white, with a halo around his head. The picture was not precisely the one from the illustrated Bible of his childhood. He had got it wrong. In the Bible, Jesus had walked on the water, not sailed in a boat.

No, what he was seeing was the miraculous draft of fishes. When he caught sight of the boat again, it was full of bearded men, hauling in a net filled with glittering silver scales.

"Come!" Jesus seemed to be saying, with scarcely a movement of his long face.

He was summoning him toward that great tract of blue, that radiant field of light, which every now and then emitted a fiercer beam that struck like an arrow between his lids.

No, that was not what He had said. It was:

"Suffer little children . . . to come unto me."

Bergelon could not quite remember. The Holy Scriptures had never been his best subject. And besides, to displace and confuse events was all part of the game. What really mattered was the desire to escape, to become someone other than oneself. How could he expect Edna to understand?

A tiny flicker of the eyelids, and the sailing boat and haloed figure disappeared. It was replaced by the beach, dotted with little pools, the narrow fringe of foam along the shore, children paddling in the shallow water, and grownups, men and women with trousers and skirts hitched up to reveal pale legs, earnestly scooping up shrimp in their nets.

Another flicker of the eyelids. Bergelon's glance, focused to exclude Edna from his line of vision—for she was irrelevant at this moment—rested on the fat girl in sugar pink, and he felt his body tingling with hot gusts of desire. It was not a conscious or rational reaction. Later on, when the girl was fully dressed again, he would feel shame. Her mother was sitting beside her in a deck chair, obese and placid, bent over her knitting; the girl, who could not have been more than fifteen or sixteen, was already almost as fat as she was. Her bathing suit, like

Edna's, was too tight. And like Edna she was lying propped up on her elbows on the sand, reading a book, quite possibly one of those Bibliothèque Rose tales for schoolgirls.

"What time is it?"

Since he was fully dressed, he could easily have looked at his watch. However, rather than come down to earth from the misty regions inhabited by the disturbing presence of the girl in pink, he replied distantly:

"I don't know."

He was unable to restore the fishing boat to its former position. In its place on the horizon, now much more sharply defined, was a steamship on its way to heaven knows where.

Where had he seen that strange-looking ship with funnels, masts, and sails, a hybrid from those early, heroic days of steam? In one of Jules Verne's novels? At any rate, it had been a black-and-white engraving or lithograph in a hardback book with the musty smell of old paper. The deck of the ship, seen from above, was littered with emigrants, huddled together among their bundles of possessions: the women in full-skirted dresses, their hair bound up in scarves, the men all bearded, and, standing alone beside the railings on the side, a young man, the hero of the story, wearing an overcoat, spats, and an immensely tall top hat.

He himself would have loved to travel on that ship, bound for the Americas.

He would also have loved to have rattled along in one of those big covered wagons that transported the pioneers to the Rocky Mountains.

"Isn't it time you had your swim?"

The mother of the fat girl had spoken. Without raising her eyes from her book, the girl replied:

"Later."

She was lingering over every line, every word, every episode, holding down the corner of the page as if she could not bear to turn it over.

Anyone watching Bergelon would have seen a fleeting shadow pass across his face. It was gone in an instant. The recollection of a small, distasteful, vaguely threatening incident. Why had he been reluctant to accompany Edna to the boule table in the casino three days before? Why had he changed his mind at the last minute? Was it because fate had decreed that he should run into Madame Jonas, the most malicious gossip in the entire parish of Saint-Nicolas? She was wearing an ash-blonde wig, of a color never to be seen in nature and of a texture that resembled cotton rather than hair.

"Doctor, are you all on your own here, without your wife?"

Then, turning to Edna, who, as if by mere chance, had latched familiarly onto Bergelon's arm:

"How do you do, madame?"

At the village school there had been a boy called Noël, who at the age of eleven was already almost as fat as the girl in pink and who walked with a pronounced waddle. He was now an estate agent in Bugle, engaged in the sale of houses and building lots. He owned a car and had several children as fat as himself.

Perhaps he, too, had never wished to be anyone other than himself. Who could tell?

The difficulty was to choose who one *did* want to be. He felt within himself a tiny tremor, in which anxiety, hope, and expectancy were mingled; he had the desire to take some decisive step. But what step? To open not so much a door as a pathway to a new world, new vistas, to rush toward . . .

He felt the thump of a beach ball on his legs, looked up, and saw that Edna had turned over onto her back and was now exposing her face to the sun, wearing huge dark glasses with milk-white rims.

He cast his mind back to all the boys he had known at school, recalling what each of them was doing now. Thioux had become a baker. He had retained his gruff voice, his heavy tread, his surly manner, and his shyness. Gallet was now a lawyer, active in politics. Occasionally, seeing Bergelon on the other side of the street, he would shout a friendly greeting:

"Hello, my dear fellow. How are you?"

The odd thing was that none of them had really changed. Now aged between thirty and thirty-five, most of them were married, with children of their own, and yet they were, for the most part, exactly as they had been when they had all been photographed together in the school playground on the occasion of the award of the Elementary Certificate of Education.

All the same, there were two or three about whom nothing was known, since they had left the neighborhood, no doubt to settle down eventually somewhere else.

His mother would be furious. He had written to her, saying that while he would ordinarily have been delighted to have her with him in Riva-Bella, he was feeling so exhausted that he was desperately in need of a little time to himself. What would she make of that, she who, like Germaine, was always ready to believe the worst?

The children would just be getting out of school. No— this was Thursday. Their mother had probably taken them into town shopping, to outfit them for the vacation.

What was so hard to determine was the extent to which the Cosson business had influenced him. Without that shameful night of the confinement, would he have been going through this present crisis, would he still have been prey to this agonizing need for change?

Had he ever really resigned himself, once and for all,

to his fate? Might it not be that his very serenity had been due precisely to the fact that he had never taken anything terribly seriously? There he was at home, in his own parish, on his own familiar streets, visiting his patients, old Hautois and the Portals, for instance, whom he had known all his life. He had the feeling that while the others were really and truly there, fixed and settled for life, he was just passing through, experiencing a temporary phase, which was scarcely more real to him than the pictures he created when he was playing shutters.

What did the Cosson business really amount to? He found it impossible to judge. He had given way to an ignoble temptation to break into the world of Mandalin and Doctor Ear-Nose-and-Throat, and perhaps, who could tell, to be able one day to afford a car of his own.

Because of this a woman and a baby had died, and life had gone on as usual, with Mandalin going to La Solonge to have lunch with friends, and Emile, having asked for and received his Sunday pocket money, setting off on a scouting expedition.

How could one pinpoint the precise moment when a suit began to feel too tight? Why that day, rather than the one before or the one after?

"Are you asleep?"

He stirred. He felt numb. His forehead, without his realizing it, was wrinkled in a frown, and his eyes were on the fat girl in pink, who, having finished her book, was now getting to her feet and tugging at her bathing suit, which was chafing her between the legs. Then she went inside the striped red-and-white tent to get her bathing cap.

"Don't go out too far."

Bergelon himself was no swimmer, though he could manage a few strokes. He wondered whether Cosson, who had never seen the sea, knew how to swim. He was stiff from having sat too long in one position. He was tempted to follow the pink bathing suit in order to watch the girl take her swim. He suspected that Edna was watching him through the smoked glass of her glasses, and so she was. With a little snigger, she said:

"Don't mind me!"

He flushed, as if caught in some shameful act. He cringed at the thought that the girl's mother might have overheard and understood, and he turned to look at her. The sun was blazing down on the jetty, the casino, and all the hotels. He was on his feet on the sand. A few seconds earlier he had been sitting with his eyes closed. Now he was about to walk down to the water's edge.

But at that very moment he glanced toward the jetty and caught sight of Germaine turning off the main road from the station, her brown suitcase in hand. She was wearing the new hat she had been trimming when he left. He remembered thinking that it was a rather odd shape. She had on one of her older dresses, for she would never dream of traveling in her good clothes, saying that nothing was more likely to ruin them than sitting in trains. Perhaps the sun was in her eyes—it was evident that she could see nothing clearly, and as she walked along looking neither right nor left, her thoughts were obviously miles away. She was probably already rehearsing what she would say to him.

"I'm going to buy some cigarettes," he announced.

"I've got some!"

"Not Gitanes . . ."

This exchange, though he did not realize it, was to be etched into his memory more deeply than anything else that had occurred between them, as was the sight of Edna pushing up her sunglasses to stare at him.

He was already walking away, weaving his way through the cabana tents and sunbathers.

Having first made sure that Germaine had disappeared from view, he set off in the opposite direction, toward the station. He was in no hurry. He felt perfectly calm. He could not remember ever having felt so calm before. Never had his mind been clearer.

It was little short of a miracle that he happened to be fully dressed: he had intended, should he have had enough of the beach, to go by bus to Deauville. For this reason, his wallet was in his inside pocket. He had left Bugle with five thousand francs on him. He had at least forty-five hundred left.

As for Germaine, she would not be left penniless. Even after he had withdrawn the five thousand francs, there were still twenty-six thousand or more left in his bank account.

He walked on, reminding himself that the local train between Riva-Bella and Caen would be returning in a few minutes. There was still time for him to walk to the end of the road, turn left, and take his place on the platform.

Twenty-six thousand francs . . . plus fees still outstanding . . . plus the few share certificates kept in the left-hand drawer of the wardrobe . . .

In addition, there was the house, which they owned, and which must be worth some hundred thousand francs.

And finally—he smiled to himself at the thought—it would be so easy to come to some arrangement about the practice. His substitute, the famous Monsieur Charles, was receiving a fixed salary of two thousand francs a month. The practice brought in about five thousand a month, seldom as little as four thousand. Say that Monsieur Charles would be content with half . . .

He started nervously at the sound of the little train's

hoarse whistle, quickened his pace, began to run, and then, when out of breath he finally reached the platform, he had at least another ten minutes to wait.

Obviously, Madame Jonas had sent a letter. Had she written directly to Germaine? Or had some third party passed on the news? Poor Germaine! She had lost no time in packing her bag. Had she confided in Monsieur Charles? He was willing to bet that she had!

And now? No doubt she had been told at the Hôtel Bellevue that he was on the beach. Was she wandering about in her town shoes, searching for him among the sunbathers?

He had no plans. It did not occur to him that there was anything special about this moment in his life. The situation seemed to him commonplace enough. He was simply fleeing the boring prospect of a scene between himself, his wife, and Edna, the absurdity of a conjugal quarrel taking place within the paper-thin walls of the hotel.

The train started up, and soon diverged from the road to run alongside the canal. Across the water, in a shady tea garden called the Robinson, couples were dancing. There were anglers fishing from the banks and motionless sailing boats, seemingly becalmed.

Cosson would flatter himself that it was on his account that Bergelon was running away. This was so far from the truth that he was determined to disprove it by sending him his address as soon as he had decided where to stay. Who could tell, perhaps the three of them would meet face to face: himself, Cosson, and Cécile.

Twenty minutes later he was stepping down from the train on Place du Marché. At this hour all the market stalls had been cleared away, leaving only the lingering smells of produce and the little bistros, now deserted, which were patronized by the market vendors.

What had made him decide to go to Le Havre? Strictly

speaking, he had made no decision. It just seemed the obvious thing to do. Since he was on the move, he would make for Le Havre, though he had not yet decided by what means of transport. To give himself time to think, he sat down at a table on the terrace of a brasserie, where there was a band playing, and ordered a glass of beer. Drinking it, he experienced the same feeling of well-being that he used to long before, on Saturday afternoons when his mother, having given him his bath and dressed him in clean clothes, allowed him to go out and roam the streets.

As he watched the comings and goings on the square, he saw a bus pull up in front of a florist's stall; he read the destination Honfleur on the side. He called the waiter and hurriedly paid his bill, once again fearful of delay, as if he had an appointment to keep. However, the bus was not due to leave for another quarter hour, and he sat in it all alone for a long time.

He had no luggage, nothing but what he was actually wearing: a pair of gray flannel trousers, an open-necked shirt, and a collarless jacket—presumably such garments had a name, but he did not know it—that he had bought the previous year in Riva-Bella. Every other man on the beach seemed to be wearing one. He did not even have his penknife with him, having left it in his bedroom; that was a nuisance, because he had sand under his nails. As he had no other means of cleaning them, he began gnawing them.

He had always had a fear of buses, which reminded him of great, clumsy bumblebees. They swerved across from one side of the road to the other, between tall hedges, overtaking powerful cars, rushing past little towns buried in the depths of the country.

He could scarcely believe it when they finally reached a town square, surrounded by old Norman buildings and bordering on a stretch of water that had motionless fishermen gazing into its depths. This was Honfleur! He had never been here before, any more than he had ever set foot in Le Havre. He approached a policeman:

"How do I get to Le Havre, please?"

The policeman looked up at the clock above the entrance to the fish market.

"You'll have an hour and a half to wait for the next ferry. . . . You would have done better to go via Tancarville."

How could he have been expected to know that? In a curious way the square reminded him of a picture in a storybook. The buildings seemed somehow unreal, and the life and bustle of the place meant nothing to him. Cars and buses came and went, to his eyes without purpose, and the fishermen, in their stiff denim clothes, remained as if rooted to the spot. It was impossible to guess why they should choose to stand there, motionless for hours, on the big stone slabs of the landing.

He went into a café. It was dark and cool inside.

There were country women in black, with children and shopping baskets, apparently waiting for something —the departure of the ferry or a coach, no doubt—and people came in laden with luggage, crates, and chicken coops, which they deposited on a table covered with oil-cloth.

Suddenly he remembered. The picture evoked by this scene was of a crowd of people waiting to board a stage-coach, in winter time though, with the travelers gathered around a blazing hearth; one of them, an Englishman, was wrapped in a tartan cape. The thing that had struck him most forcibly had been the tartan cape. For a long time after, he had longed to possess a tartan cape, but the opportunity had never arisen.

"Some cider, please."

"Bottled?"

He did not understand the question.

"That'll do nicely."

As soon as the words were out of his mouth, he felt inclined to call back the waitress, whose weary eyes suggested that she could do with a good night's sleep. He was suddenly in the grip of an emotion not unlike avarice. He ought, he felt, to have asked the price of a bottle of cider. How long would his forty-five hundred francs last at this rate?

The girl was wearing a black wool dress under a white apron. She was bustling back and forth, collecting glasses, wiping the brown oilcloth tablecloths with a rag, and being constantly interrupted in her work by people asking questions:

"No, there isn't another bus to Tancarville until eight o'clock. . . ."

If Mile were here with him, he thought, he would be sitting silent and motionless in some dark corner. That was his way whenever he found himself in unfamiliar surroundings, faced with sights that were new to him. He seemed to be in a daze. Then weeks or even months later, when reference was made to this place or that, he would suddenly break in:

"The walls were painted blue, not green, and there was a calendar above the fireplace that had a picture of a harvest scene."

"Do you have a telephone, mademoiselle?"

"Over there, on the left."

A telephone fixed to the wall in the passage at the back, next to a urinal that reeked of ammonia.

"Would you please put me through to Riva-Bella 28."

"With recall!" barked the proprietress, who had suddenly appeared from nowhere.

He had no idea what she meant. Still holding the receiver, he stared at her, bemused.

Nevertheless, he repeated to the operator: "With re-call!"

"Replace the receiver. I'll call you back."

"What does 'with recall' mean?"

"That the operator is to call back and let me know the length of the call."

So be it! "With recall," by all means! He had no objection. He was taking this course less for Germaine's sake —she now seemed as far away as if he were seeing her through the wrong end of a telescope—than to avoid an unpleasant scene. He would not be there to witness it, of course. He could simply have washed his hands of it. But he could not banish the thought of his wife fainting in the foyer of the hotel, surrounded by a crowd of onlookers passing through on their way to the dining room, and the very idea was distasteful to him.

"Would you believe it! Her husband . . ."

"Let us hope he hasn't drowned himself! Men are so impulsive. . . ."

And Edna, right in the midst of it all! Edna, whom he had left on the pretext of going to buy cigarettes! Would the two women come face to face? The sun was already setting. Sooner or later, the two of them would have to go into the dining room for dinner, to be served by the three waitresses, who made the wooden floorboards shake as they stomped about handing out the dishes.

"Your call to Riva-Bella."

"Thanks.

"Hello, is this the Hôtel Bellevue? . . . I wonder if you could tell me whether Madame Bergelon has arrived yet?"

He was put through to another extension. A woman's voice, that of the daughter of the proprietress, who had been giving him some odd looks ever since she caught sight of Edna coming out of his room, asked:

"Who is calling?"

He could hear what he took to be footsteps coming and going in the visitors' lounge. He was anxious for fear that the ferry would leave without him.

"Is Madame Bergelon in the hotel?"

"Do you wish me to call her to the phone? She has just gone in to dinner."

He had momentarily forgotten how early dinner was served, to enable those guests who wished to go to the movies to get there by half past eight.

"No! . . . Hello! . . . Don't cut me off! . . ."

"Continue!" interposed the switchboard operator. "You haven't been cut off."

"Hello, is this the Hôtel Bellevue? . . . Would you please give a message to Madame Bergelon . . . No! . . . There's no need to call her to the phone. . . ."

For a voice at the other end had announced:

"She's just coming. . . ."

He could picture the scene. The daughter of the proprietress had no doubt shouted to one of the waitresses:

"Tell Madame Bergelon she's wanted on the telephone. . . ."

And poor Germaine scrambling to her feet . . .

And Edna watching her as she made her way to the door . . .

And all the hotel guests enthralled by the drama of the lady whose husband . . .

"Hello. Just give her this message: her husband is well. . . . Yes. . . . He's been called away unexpectedly . . . just for a few days, to . . . to Dieppe. . . . That's right!"

His head was buzzing. Before replacing the receiver, he had heard a voice that he recognized as his wife's, quite close to the instrument, asking:

"Is it my husband?"

He hung up. He was mopping the perspiration from his forehead when the telephone rang again. He dared not lift the receiver, fearful lest . . .

"Hello, Honfleur 12? . . . Six minutes to Riva-Bella . . ."

"Five francs fifty!" snapped the proprietress.

Through the window, he could see the ferryboat at the dock, with cars driving up the ramp.

"What do I owe you?"

"Five-fifty for the phone call, and two francs for the cider . . . seven-fifty . . ."

He handed over ten francs and went out. No sooner had he done so than he began to regret having left a tip of two francs fifty. At this rate . . .

Dusk was beginning to fall. He was crushed among the crowd of passengers. The funnel of the ferry reminded him of the paddleboat on the deck of which . . .

He felt a sudden sharp pang, a stab of hope, a sensation as if a bubble of air were trapped in his lungs. As he gazed down at the calm, glittering water, motionless but for the patches of garbage floating lazily on the undertow, tears came into his eyes, as if he were going away forever, as if the Honfleur ferry were equipped for . . .

"Tickets, please."

Soon, the moment it was quite dark, Eveline Portal would be out on the porch. It had never occurred to him to wonder whether Germaine, at the age of sixteen or seventeen, had gone in for games of that sort with boys. . . . It was not impossible. . . . It was even probable! Trembling, as was her wont, hiding her face in her hands, struggling to hold back her tears.

As if they were really in the open sea, there were gulls flying in the wake of the boat. A woman turned to her husband and asked:

"How much did you pay?"

And Bergelon saw that the tip of his cigarette was quivering. He had great difficulty lighting it. He had to bend down, sheltering behind the backs of other passengers, because a light breeze was blowing, extinguishing each match as he struck it.

Chapter Eight

 E ven before disembarking he was conscious of an uncongenial atmosphere. Was it because he was seeing the town for the first time in that dusky gloom midway between day and night? The sun had vanished from the sky, there was no pink afterglow, no trace of blue or green. What color was it, in fact? No color. It was like frosted glass, and beneath it everything looked dingy. The houses, the windows, the doors were sharply defined, as in an etching, in harsh browns and hard, steely grays.

He hated Le Havre. He detested everything about it, its streetcars, its architecture, the rhythms of its streets. But was rhythm the right word? Scarcely. It seemed at this hour almost a dead town, with only one or two people returning home late, sidewalks too broad for the few people using them; the place was already lighted, although it was not yet dark, by gas lamps. As for the waterfront itself, it consisted of nothing but sheds, iron gates, and billboards covered with hideous posters that announced the forthcoming arrival of a circus.

No, this was not what he was looking for. He must move on at once. Although it was the dinner hour, he could not face the thought of staying in the town long enough to have a meal. He seemed to be afraid that something would detain him, that if he lingered here, he would never be able to get away, to do what he had to do.

What was it that he had to do? He had no idea. He had not given it a thought. When he was in a conveyance of any sort, he invariably ceased to think. He merely waited.

Possibly there was some other cause for his irrational antipathy toward Le Havre. Just before disembarking, as the other passengers were already jostling him forward to the exit at the front of the ferry, he was struck with a thought so obvious that it seemed absurd that it had not occurred to him before.

When he had telephoned the Hôtel Bellevue he had asked that his wife should be told. This was an admission that he knew that Germaine was there, from which it would not be hard to deduce that he had seen her in Riva-Bella and had promptly taken flight. And yet all he need have said was:

"Doctor Bergelon speaking. . . . If anyone asks for me . . ."

What he had actually said might have ugly consequences. What was Germaine going to think? That he was frightened of her? This was enough to show him in an unflattering—one might almost say a dissolute—light, whereas in fact his flight had had nothing to do with his wife's arrival, nor with anything else that had occurred that afternoon on the beach.

How could one be sure that she would be able to contain herself? Suppose she burst into tears in front of all those people?

"That's the wife of that little doctor fellow. . . . She's just found out that her husband . . ."

And everyone would turn to stare at Edna.

"Excuse me, monsieur, can you tell me if the last bus for Saint-Valéry has left yet?" a respectable-looking woman asked the ticket collector, who replied:

"There's one leaving in a few minutes. You'd better hurry."

Bergelon followed her. She was carrying a black wicker basket in one hand and a bundle in the other. He was tempted to offer to help carry them, but he feared that she might think it odd.

To hell with it! He would go to Saint-Valéry. The lights were on in the bus. In the beam of the headlights a house would suddenly appear, or a group of people standing in a dark corner on the opposite side of the road. Every now and then the bus would stop in front of a grocer's or a café.

The bus was going all the way to Dieppe, and Bergelon remained on it, one of only three or four passengers left. Smoking was forbidden, which irked him.

He would have to stop somewhere, but not in Dieppe, particularly as that was the town that he had named in his telephone message. He could not see the sea, but there was a lighthouse beam circling in the sky as they drove along the coast road, and lights, strung out like necklaces, divided the town from the total darkness beyond. The bus stopped behind a row of other buses, all of different colors.

As people were climbing into one of them, he asked the conductor:

"Where are you going?"

"Abbeville."

He got on. It was late. It was growing chilly. He had never been to Abbeville. He had no desire to go there. Still, who could tell? He might find some other means of transport there, and . . .

And that was how he came to be in Boulogne at one o'clock in the morning. He was suddenly conscious of the heaving of his stomach, brought on by hunger, and he ate a plate of *choucroute garnie* in a brasserie, which was deserted except for four men playing cards. He had no idea whether he was in the center of the town or on the outskirts. The streets were as gloomy as those of Le Havre.

"Is there a hotel near here?"

"Two houses along. . . . Keep your finger on the bell, because the proprietor is hard of hearing."

He was asleep as soon as his head touched the pillow. When he awoke he found that his watch had stopped. Thinking that he had overslept, he got dressed, went downstairs, and found himself on an empty street at six o'clock in the morning. Once again he was well away from the sea; walking on, he found himself on a square where market stalls were being erected.

Then he thought of Antwerp. The name just suddenly came into his mind, and he did not reject it. He went on toward the railroad station and made inquiries at the information desk. He was more than a little daunted by the unexpected complications involved. Apparently, there was no direct train to Antwerp. He would have to backtrack as far as Lille, then spend three hours there waiting for a connection.

He could still not get over his clumsy handling of the telephone call. How could he have failed to foresee the consequences of that message of his?

He had lunch in Lille, though he could not have said

afterward where or what he had eaten. Fortunately, he had his identity card in his wallet. He would be required to produce it at the border.

He could have stopped in Brussels. He had never been to Brussels either. But it had become an obsession with him: he was going to Antwerp!

Once there, it would happen. What would happen, he neither knew nor cared. That would look after itself, once he had arrived in Antwerp.

And arrive he did, at ten o'clock in the evening. Immediately, emerging from the central station, he felt a sense of well-being at the sight of a brilliantly lighted boulevard, alive with warm, breathing human beings.

At last he could call a halt, breathe in the atmosphere, look about him. He enjoyed listening to the passers-by talking Flemish. It was as if not being able to understand them was an added pleasure. He walked about the streets, feeling sorely tempted to talk aloud to himself.

"No," he murmured to himself, stopping outside a restaurant. "There must be better ones than this."

He was sure in his own mind that this avenue must lead to the docks, and he had already decided that the docks were where he wanted to go.

His eye was caught by the façade of another restaurant. It was an odd-looking place, with the bill of fare written in large letters on the windows in white paint. Inside, ovens were lined up along the whole of one wall. A man in a white chef's hat was bustling busily about. Though it was far from elegant, there was a noisy friendliness about the place that appealed to him. He went in and sat down at a marble-topped table, breathing in the thick fumes of frying grease.

"Mussels for one, one! Two portions of fries! One shrimp salad!"

"What can I get you?"

The waiter, wiping his table with a dirty cloth, pushed the greasy menu toward him.

"Mussels!" he ordered.

It was odd that he should come to rest, as it were, before a bowl of mussels, for mussels had always been a bone of contention in his family life. He could not think of any dish he enjoyed more than mussels. The same was true of his son. Both of them would have liked nothing better than to have them two or three times a week. Unfortunately, however, neither Germaine nor Annie liked them. And besides, Germaine, who was afraid of everything, feared that they might be poisoned.

From now on he was going to be able to stuff himself with mussels to his heart's content! He was served a huge portion in a brown enamel casserole. They were enormous, of an appetizing ivory color, of a firm and yet tender consistency, and flavored with onions and celery.

He recalled that on the rare occasions Germaine cooked mussels she did not include celery.

There were not many people in the restaurant, for it was past the normal dinner hour and still too early for the crowds coming out of the movie houses and theaters. Just across the way was a large movie house, lit up with violet fluorescent strips, with an auditorium as vast as the interior of a temple or a bank.

As he ate he stacked the blue-black shells in a bowl that had been placed on the table beside him. It was a long time before he noticed the woman sitting alone at a corner table facing his, eating a sirloin steak with fries.

When at last he glanced at her, she returned his look. At once he thought to himself:

"Why not?"

She understood. This was evident because after a brief interval she looked at him again, with a hint of questioning in her placid glance.

What appealed to him was that she was as plump as the girl in the pink bathing suit, with the same white skin, all curves and dimples. She was older, of course, but could not have been more than about twenty-two. She was savoring her food. Every now and then she would pause to glance up at him. She was not sure yet whether he had any serious intentions. She looked placid, sweet-natured and easygoing, no doubt a typical Flemish girl, with a turned-up nose, prominent, light-blue eyes, and a mouth curved in a slight, natural smile.

He winked at her and thought he detected some response, but he was not sure.

"What would you like next?" asked the waiter.

He hesitated, noting that it would be at least ten minutes before the woman finished eating, and ordered a second portion of mussels.

It was a stroke of luck, coming upon a pretty, plump Flemish girl like this at the first opportunity. He was drinking beer, which tasted different from any obtainable in France. He paid for his meal, astonished to find how cheap it was, watching the woman all the while. He waited for her to leave, then followed her out of the restaurant and found her waiting for him a few yards away. It was as if it had been decreed from the beginning of time that they should meet.

Her first words, spoken with disarming frankness, were:

"Where shall we go?"

He had not considered the question. He replied that he had no idea.

"You're French, aren't you?"

"Yes."

"Have you booked into a hotel?"

"Not yet."

She looked at him in some surprise, perhaps because

he had no luggage. And it was indeed somewhat unusual to see a man arriving from abroad in what could only be described as beachwear, without even a hat.

"We'll go to the Globe," she decided. "It's a bit more expensive than some, but at least it's clean."

As he walked beside her he was reminded of Cécile, whom he had often seen turning off onto a side street in company with a stranger, exactly as he and the Flemish girl were doing now. The side street was dark. The only lights were a sign over a garage in the distance and, nearer at hand, a round, milky globe with HOTEL painted on it. Beneath was an open door that led to a dimly lighted foyer.

"You'd better pay in advance," advised his companion.

They were shown to a room by a weary chambermaid, who did not even glance at them and who fumbled under her apron for change, which she kept in a purse attached to her belt.

"Do you come from Paris?"

He did not reply at once. He was frowning. Without warning he was seized with cramps in the chest and stomach, accompanied by nausea. Meanwhile, the girl was undressing, folding her clothes with care. He noticed that she was wearing an elastic girdle, which cut into the bottom of her bulging buttocks.

"Aren't you going to undress?"

He hesitated, then, unwisely, began taking off his clothes. He had always had a weak stomach. He had eaten too many mussels.

"Is this your first visit to Antwerp?"

Yes, of course it was! Good God, couldn't she stop bothering him for a minute? He was desperately in need of a little peace and quiet. Thinking that he might feel better lying down than standing up, he stretched out on the bed beside her. Then she said something stupid:

"Aren't you going to get yourself ready?"

At that moment he was forced to leap out of bed, rush to the sink, and vomit. With a wave of his hand he ordered her to be silent, knowing that otherwise she would chatter endlessly in that exasperatingly placid voice of hers.

"I thought at the time that you shouldn't be eating all those mussels."

And she lay there, waiting for him! She just lay there, gazing up at the ceiling, listening to him retching!

He went to the window, opened it, and leaned on the sill, staring at the deserted sidewalks in the luminous glow from the avenue.

"Aren't you feeling any better? If you don't put something on, you'll catch cold."

He was in a furious temper, besides feeling really ill. The sight of that white naked body stretched out on the bed filled him with nausea.

"For God's sake, shut up!" he shouted.

"Very well, if that's how you want it. As a rule, Frenchmen have better manners."

And she did manage to keep her mouth shut for a couple of minutes. But soon it became too much for her:

"If you must have the window open, you might at least draw the curtains. . . . What if a policeman saw you? . . . I'd be the one who'd get in trouble!"

"Listen . . ." he began, turning toward her.

He hesitated. No, really, it was the best way.

"Get dressed. I'm feeling ill. I'd prefer to be left alone."

"Well, really! You're some customer!"

Would Cécile, in a similar situation, have spoken so coarsely?

"The room has been booked for the night, hasn't it? Are you suggesting that I should get dressed, find myself another room, and pay for it?"

For Christ's sake, he was the one who had paid for the room, wasn't he?

He could feel that he was about to be sick again. He wanted to be alone. He fumbled in his wallet. The bills rustled, and she could see that he was carrying a lot of money.

"Here, take this. Get dressed, and get out!"

"Fifty francs? Are you crazy? And besides, this is French money."

What had made him so tightfisted all of a sudden? Why could he not give her a hundred francs? It would be well worth it, to get rid of her.

"That's enough! Get out!"

"So that's your idea of good manners, is it? Fifty francs! And by now the streetcars aren't even running. Am I expected to pay for a taxi, on top of everything else?"

He was going to be sick. He must get rid of her, and quickly.

"Here! There's ten francs for the taxi."

"Ten francs! Just you wait while I call the manager. She'll tell you I'm not in the habit of . . ."

He could no longer hear her. He was bending over the sink. He was aware that she was at least getting dressed, though not for a second did she cease protesting.

"Next time a Frenchman . . ."

He could not remember whether he had put his wallet back in his pocket. All he needed, on top of everything else, was to be robbed! Eventually, however, he spotted his wallet on the dressing table, and he went across to get it.

"I don't know what you take me for, but . . ."

He could still hear her, outside on the landing, talking vehemently to the chambermaid.

He crossed the room and locked the door. He lay

down. Then, noticing that he had forgotten to turn off the light, he had to get up again. Later, after the lights on the avenue had been turned off, he got out of bed once more, this time to shut the window because he was beginning to feel cold.

What finally prevented him from getting any further sleep was the sound of pails of water being sloshed onto the road. Then the swishing of a broom, back and forth endlessly on the paving stones. All that remained of the previous night's attack of nausea was a slight feeling of weakness in all his limbs.

He had not shaved the previous day. He had no razor and no shaving soap. He washed as well as he could and resolved to go to a barber.

A chambermaid, not the same one as last night, was scrubbing the tiles in the foyer of the hotel. There were more women out in the street, scrubbing the doorsteps. It was a clear day. The light was so bright and sharp that the rays of the sun seemed to pierce his eyelids like needles. Sounds from near and far blended like the instruments of an orchestra, the most dominant being the rumble of wagon wheels on cobblestones, the slow hammering of horses' hooves, and the shrill whistle of streetcars.

For a second, as he walked past a grocer's stall and breathed in the scent of freshly picked greens and ripe fruit, he felt suddenly transported back to Bugle on a market day. The impression was so strong that he almost expected to run into Germaine, with her string shopping bag over her arm, accompanying Emile to school. The arrival of a brewer's dray at the door of a café strengthened the illusion, bringing with it a whiff of Portal's yard, vibrant with sunlight and rural smells.

At the end of a little passageway, without warning, he suddenly saw masts, the red-ringed funnel of a steamer, a skeletal iron crane surrounded by a cloud of bluish steam flecked with gold.

He was in Antwerp! He could see himself there, as if he were standing next to himself, looking on. What he could see was a rather short man of slim build walking about the streets with a spring in his step, looking around in amazement.

Coming upon a brass shaving bowl hanging above a door, he went in, sat down in a barber's chair, tucked a paper towel under his chin, and saw his own face staring at him across the room.

Soon only his head was visible above the gown that enveloped him and the rolls of toweling wrapped around his neck. It seemed an unnaturally small head, which soon disappeared under a mass of white foam—first the cheeks, then the chin, until all that was left were the two dark discs that were his eyes.

This was the time of day when the Hôtel Bellevue was buzzing with people coming and going, with children shrieking. People calling up the stairs telling their kids to hurry up, rushing here and there, searching for a lost deck chair or toy, the guests asking one another questions, discussing the events of the day, seeking information about the state of the tide.

"Has your husband arrived yet?"

"He's coming on the 11:15 train."

Was Germaine still there? Or had she already left? In either event, she had got herself into a ludicrous situation. Especially since everyone in the hotel probably knew her story and felt sorry for her!

The wife of the man who had slunk off without telling a soul.

Who could tell? Perhaps she and Edna had spoken. They were quite capable of it! He could just imagine Edna saying at the top of her voice:

"I can assure you, I wouldn't lift a finger to take him away from you."

And Germaine, he could see her, too, with her handkerchief crumpled into a ball in her hand, flushed with embarrassment, not knowing where to look, saying her piece:

"Listen, madame . . . I know it's not your fault. . . . You have a son. . . . You will understand my position. . . . I have two children. . . . It's for their sake that . . ."

The maddening thing was that both of them had got the wrong end of the stick. What had happened had nothing whatsoever to do with either of them. He had fled because . . .

"Could you turn your head a little to the right, please?"

He did so, at the same time endeavoring not to lose sight of his reflection in the mirror.

The urge to leave might just as easily have come upon him six months or even two years earlier!

What would be really unjust would be to equate him with that fellow from the Vosges—or was it the Jura?—the timber merchant, Monsieur Charles's father, whose wife was such a perfect lady, with her white hair, mild manners, and kindly disposition.

Besides, he had no intention of shirking his obligations to his wife and children. He would be sending them money as soon as he started earning again. There was no reason for them to be unhappy. Nothing was going to change Germaine, whether he was there or not. In fact, she would be better off. She was never more in her element than when she had cause for complaint! She would be able to sigh and weep to her heart's content, all alone in her kitchen. She would be able to count every penny, and pinch and save, and comfort herself with the thought that she was the worthiest of women.

As for Annie, she would make the most of the opportunity for impressing her friends:

"My father left us without a word to anyone, you
know."

What Mile would miss most was his Sunday pocket
money. . . . But at least he had his Scout tent. . . .

He could almost hear him on the stairs on a Sunday
morning, with his hobnailed shoes and his heavy tread,
which somehow always seemed heavier on that day.

"Do you want a hair conditioner?"

He said yes, not because he needed it but because it
gave him an excuse for sitting there a little while longer.
A young apprentice was sweeping the floor of the barber-
shop. Another was polishing the nickel-plated instruments. Through the open door the street noises could be
clearly heard. In the next chair a man was being given a
scalp massage. He was clearly a man of substance, a man
not unlike Portal, almost certainly the boss of some big
commercial concern. He was smoking a cigar, which had
beautiful blue-white ash on the end. His eyes were half
shut on account of the smoke. He was obviously a regular. They knew what he wanted done and what kind of
hair lotion he liked best.

"There you are, then, Monsieur de Koening."

He was a fine-looking man. He smelled good. His gray,
lightweight suit was well fitted, just loose enough to sit
easily on his bulky frame. He was pleased with himself,
looking forward to a good day. He would enjoy an excel-
lent lunch. No doubt he, too, had a wife and children and
lived in one of those spacious houses Bergelon had seen
in the town, with sparkling windows, draped muslin curtains, and a stretch of sidewalk in front, washed and
scrubbed.

"Thank you, Monsieur de Koening."

As for himself, the assistant merely asked indifferently:

"Anything else I can do for you?"

"No, thank you."

Once again he took his wallet, containing forty-five hundred francs, from his inside pocket. While they were changing a hundred French francs for him his eye was caught by a calendar hanging on the wall. Realizing that it was Wednesday, his mind strayed involuntarily to the boulevard leading to the hospital, with all the little soldiers in battle dress under the shady trees, and the phalanx of prostitutes stretching right back to the town center. Superintendent Grosclaude, with his strutting walk, his leisurely manner of puffing at his pipe and of looking at people from under his overhanging eyebrows, was another one who created an impression of discreet self-satisfaction.

"Didn't you bring a hat?"

No, he did not have a hat. What need was there for him to wear a hat, now that he was no longer Doctor Bergelon?

No sooner was he out of the barber's than the sun took possession of him, enveloping him as it enveloped everything—people, objects, and buildings—transforming the town and life itself into a joyful symphony. He was free to turn right or left, it made no difference, but the docks were to the right, he could smell them. The policemen were wearing white caps and white gloves. The cars seemed to him bigger, shinier, and quieter than those in France. There was a great deal of scrubbing, washing, and polishing going on everywhere. Windows, metalwork, and doorsteps all gleamed in the sun. The ships' sirens sounded continually, and there were occasional loud crashes, as if one of the cranes had collapsed.

In his bedroom above the shoemaker's, Cosson had probably only just gotten out of bed. Still unwashed and half asleep, his eyes bleary, a foul aftertaste of spirits in his mouth, he would be standing at the window, looking down onto the dingy street where the upholsterer sat on the sidewalk carding wool for his mattresses.

Perhaps he had written to him again? If so, had the letter been waiting for him at the Hôtel Bellevue when Germaine checked in? As a rule Germaine scrupulously avoided opening his letters. It was one of her little affectations. Instead, she would hover at his side while he read them, watching him inquisitively all the while.

But *that* letter she must surely have opened! What had Cosson had to say? What would she make of it?

Suddenly realizing that he was feeling hungry, he went into what he took to be a little café, having so far seen nothing resembling a French bar, with its basket of croissants on the counter.

Once inside, he felt utterly out of his element. At first, the dark room, with its highly polished oak paneling and leather armchairs, seemed deserted. Then a respectable-looking woman slipped silently behind the counter and asked him, first in Flemish, then in French, what she could do for him.

"Would it be possible to have something to eat?"

"One moment."

She disappeared. From a small adjoining pantry he could hear the clatter of plates and the slicing of some kind of foodstuff. This went on for about five minutes.

Then, at last, he heard her call "Edgar!" to someone at the back.

A young man, wearing black trousers and a white apron, which he was still fastening, glanced around the café.

"Would you serve that gentleman? Ask him what he wants to drink."

Edgar brought Bergelon a dish filled with slices of ham, sausage, and Dutch cheese, then another piled with very white, close-textured bread, a jar of mustard, and a lined butter dish with an outer compartment packed with ice.

If Germaine . . .

He could just imagine her gazing at this spread with mingled fascination and disapproval.

"What would you like to drink?"

"Have you any wine?"

"Moselle?"

The Moselle, greenish and a little sour, was served in a long-stemmed glass. The proprietress and Edgar stood whispering in the pantry, taking turns coming to have another look at this freak.

Never in all his life had he eaten such an extraordinary breakfast. The café was divided from the street, not by large glass windows but by leaded panes of bottle glass, which distorted everything in sight. The room was cool and just sufficiently dim to give it an agreeable atmosphere of mystery. In the pantry something was frying, but he could not guess from the smell what it might be. Sausage, perhaps? For a moment he wondered whether it was for him, but nothing was said about it. Perhaps it was Edgar's breakfast.

"What do I owe you?"

"Eighteen francs seventy-five."

It was a lot of money. Oh, well, never mind! This recent onset of meanness surprised him. As he walked along in the direction of the Steen he concentrated on working out exactly what he had spent since his departure. More than three hundred francs already!

Before him lay the Scheldt, very broad and glittering with tiny flecks of light in the wake of passing tugs and motorboats. A few cargo vessels lay at anchor. Bergelon was mildly disappointed to see so few ships, so little hustle and bustle.

It was not until he had been walking for almost an hour that he realized that the big ships were moored elsewhere, in what seemed to him a maze of interconnected docks.

He was in Antwerp! He was not unhappy! He did not feel a complete outsider! Indeed, the fact that he was an outsider—he was reminded of it every time he overheard Flemish being spoken—actually delighted him.

What pained him a little—no, pained was too strong a word, rather say irritated and bewildered him—was that none of this seemed quite real to him. He had a feeling that at any moment . . .

It had been the same at Riva-Bella. The beach had seemed just as unreal, and so had Edna and the fat girl in pink.

So, what *was* real? His big-wheeled bike, on which he made most of his rounds, his consulting room with the door that he opened to let out each patient in turn, peering into the dim waiting room to see who was next? Madame Pholien and her stomach troubles? The children with mumps . . . ?

"I'm sure he must have written to me," he thought.

Germaine would certainly have read the letter and would have understood not a word of it. Like Edna— what a name!—when he had asked her if she had ever wished she could change places with someone else.

That was the one thing that he was unable to do. He walked and walked, and everything about him was strange and novel, and yet never for a moment could he forget the familiar sights and sounds of home: the clearing where they had picnicked a couple of weeks ago to try out Mile's tent . . . the boulevard leading to the hospital . . . the farmyard by the river front, which he had to cross to visit old Hautois. . . . Perhaps Hautois had taken advantage of his absence to die. . . . Who could tell? If so, no one would know, because no one but Bergelon ever bothered to climb the steep stairs to his little attic room.

As for Madame Portal, with her jealousy, and with her legs immersed in that enamel basin . . .

"Excuse me, sir, I wonder if you could tell me whether, by any chance, you have a vacancy for a doctor aboard one of your ships?"

That was the last thing he wanted! He could not see himself going into one of those offices full of mahogany furniture that were to be found in all the buildings along the waterfront . . . Cunard Line . . . Messageries Maritimes . . . Compagnie Transatlantique de . . . Compagnie d'Exploitations Minières du Haut-Congo . . . Société Forestière de . . .

To change places . . . to become someone else! He, who could scarcely refrain from blushing when anyone he knew turned to look at him, surprised because he was wearing a bathing suit!

He had never walked so far in all his life. He kept losing his way, especially in the dock area, constantly finding himself back where he had started, opposite a Dutch bank, a tall narrow building towering above the single-story café next to it.

The girls would by now be leaving the hospital. Accompanying them as far as the end of the boulevard would be Superintendent Grosclaude, pushing his bicycle with one hand and holding his lighted pipe in the other, walking with long, slow, even strides, like the swing of a pendulum.

Good God! Suddenly, as in a flash of lightning, he could see himself as he had been the very first time he had made up his mind to run away. It was when he was thirteen and in the fifth grade at the lycée. There he stood, watching a boat discharge a cargo of wooden planks from faraway places. He had been learning about the Peloponnesian War, and he had stolen a hundred-franc note from his father's wallet, intending to make for Le Havre, yes, Le Havre, the town that now seemed to him so ugly. Then one morning he had put on three shirts, one on top of the other, and stuffed his pockets and satchel with everything they could hold.

In the end he had not run away, he could no longer remember why. Having no further use for the hundred francs, they had been an embarrassment to him. He had not dared to return them to his father's wallet, still less to spend them. He had been tempted to give the note to a poor blind man who lived in the parish of Saint-Nicolas, but had realized that this was too risky.

For months he had kept the note, rolled up like a cigarette, on the top of a wardrobe, hidden behind the cornice. For months he had tormented himself every night on account of that note.

At last, one day he had retrieved it from its hiding place—it was a Thursday, and the waters of the Loire were swollen—and wrapped it around a pebble. At the last minute he had taken the added precaution of tying his handkerchief around it with string before hurling it as far as he was able into the swirling water.

Weeks later, when the level of the water had fallen, he went out of his way to return to the spot, to make sure that his handkerchief was not visible on the gravel bed of the river!

He went into a notions store that also sold postcards. He had his fountain pen with him.

Addressing one card to Bugle, he wrote:

> Don't worry. Everything is fine.
> Father

And on the other:

> Everything is fine.
> Love,
> Elie

This card he addressed to Germaine Bergelon, Hôtel Bellevue.

He had bought three cards. He had begun addressing the third when he thought better of it. Deciding in the end that he ought to give himself time to reflect, he slipped the postcard, already stamped, into his pocket.

Chapter Nine

His visit to the Cristal-Palace and his meeting with Clarius occurred on his third day in Antwerp. Nothing had changed during those three days, except that Bergelon had in the interval made himself at home.

He was no longer merely a man passing through, but a boarder, thanks to the landlady of the Oude Antwerp. Strolling along the waterfront, he had noticed this building, more picturesque than the others by virtue of its fretted gable and its narrow windows decorated with gilding. Was it a genuinely old house? He was not sure. Old or not, however, the words "Oude Antwerp," meaning Old Antwerp, were carved in Gothic lettering above the door.

Having ascertained that it was a rooming house, he had gone inside. He had asked for a room and had been subjected to close scrutiny by the landlady, who had then asked:

"For how long?"

He had felt uneasy, not so much on account of the question as because of the familiarity with which the woman looked him up and down. It reminded him of the way some mothers turn their babies this way and that to see how they are progressing. He had a feeling that as far as he was concerned she had weighed him and found him wanting.

"We don't rent rooms for less than a week, because here, you understand, every room is thoroughly turned out before rerenting."

She climbed the stairs hesitantly, stopping from time to time as if reluctant to take him in.

"And besides, you know, it is forbidden to entertain women in the bedrooms at night. If you wish to entertain a female relative, you are welcome to use the sitting room downstairs."

In the end she had no choice but to open one of the doors. The room, with its oak furniture and ornaments, was more like a bedroom in a private house than a hotel room.

"When will you be bringing your luggage?"

He flushed, then stammered some vague excuse. And as he was going out to fetch his nonexistent luggage from God knows where, the woman made one final effort to put him off.

"I must also warn you that we don't serve breakfast in the bedrooms, as is the custom in France. A meal consisting of coffee, rolls, and boiled eggs is available in the dining room."

He went out and bought a suitcase. As soon as he got it outside, it struck him that the landlady might easily find out that there was nothing in it. He did not want to spend money, but he had already set his heart on that rooming house.

It was then that he spotted a secondhand bookshop. He went in and bought several old books, choosing the biggest and heaviest he could find. One of them was in Latin and another in Flemish, but they were cheap, and that was all that mattered. He had bought thirty francs' worth of books in all, and the case was heavy. Next he bought a razor—a bargain—some shaving soap, and a cheap shaving brush. He was still finding it hard to part with any of the money he had. All the same, he resigned himself to the necessity of two shirts and two pairs of socks.

He had a confused sense that this was no way to behave; he nevertheless steeled himself to make these purchases.

That afternoon he wrote to Germaine. Another postcard. It was so much easier than a letter.

> Don't worry. All is well.
> Love,
> Elie

He addressed the card to Riva-Bella, although it was more than likely that his wife had returned home to Bugle by now. With this in mind, he wrote a second card, this one addressed to Emile and Annie:

> Everything is fine. Perfect weather.
> Your loving father

That night he went to bed early. Next morning, after wandering about the town for a while, he went into a post office, drafted several telegrams to Cosson—which he tore to shreds one after the other—and finally settled on the following curt message:

> Am in Antwerp. Bergelon.

He did not have the courage to add his address. If Cosson wanted to write to him, he could always send the letter poste restante.

It was the same evening that he followed the young ladies of the Salvation Army. He dined all alone in a very ordinary restaurant. He attached great importance to everything he did, as if to endow all his actions with greater significance, whereas he knew in his heart that none of this bore any relation either to his past or to his future. A young woman wearing the uniform of the Salvation Army had been distributing tracts. She had put one on Bergelon's table, and he had given her a franc, at the same time raising his head and looking at her.

He had gone on eating, following her with his eyes as she went from table to table. By the time she went out he had not yet finished his cheese. Perhaps the memory of her lingered in his mind. A quarter of an hour later he left the restaurant. At any rate, standing outside on the sidewalk, he could not decide what to do next. The truth was that he would have liked to go to a movie, but this notion seemed to him somehow absurd and inappropriate. By now, all the lights in the town were on. He walked on until he came to an intersection. He was just about to cross the street when he saw the Salvation Army girl again, this time in company with two others, also in uniform.

With them was a uniformed man, probably an officer. At any rate, something about his smooth though not very well-shaved face, his grayish coloring, his dull eyes, his air of a man resolutely dedicated to duty, reminded Bergelon of his former company sergeant major.

A streetcar pulled up. The three young women got on, and he, not quite knowing why, followed them. The streetcar was of a design until now unfamiliar to him, the seating being in the form of two long benches facing each other. The yellowish lights dimmed every time the car crossed cables. Through the windows could be seen rows of little shops on suburban streets, deserted at this hour, with here and there whole families sitting on chairs outside on the sidewalk.

The streetcar stopped and started up again every hundred yards or so, whether or not there was anyone wanting to get on or off. Bergelon had no idea where it was going. He was alone on one of the long benches, and the three young women were huddled together on the bench opposite, although there was space for at least fifteen people. They were in a huddle like schoolgirls exchanging secrets, and were in fact whispering and smiling, and in the end, in spite of every effort to contain themselves, giggling unrestrainedly. At this point they looked at him uneasily, as if by their laughter they had committed some gross indiscretion.

He wished he could hear what they were saying. Two of them could not have been much over thirty, but the third, a good deal thinner than the others, must have been well on in her forties. From time to time he caught the odd word. From his platform the conductor looked at them without interest, no doubt thinking only that he would soon be at the end of his day's work.

That was all there was to it. Somewhere, in a sparsely populated district where there were only a few lighted windows to be seen, the three women got off. He lacked the courage to follow them. He watched them as they paused on the corner and exchanged a few words. Then the oldest of the three set off in one direction and the other two, arm in arm, in the opposite direction.

He was the only passenger aboard when the streetcar reached the end of the line.

That was how he had passed the time that evening. He could have stayed on the streetcar and gone back into town, but he was afraid of what the conductor might think as he sat, taking advantage of this brief respite, to eat a thick slice of bread with butter, stuffing it into his mouth until his cheeks bulged. He had first opened a compartment and taken out a small blue container that presumably held coffee.

As for Bergelon, he had roamed about aimlessly while awaiting the next streetcar. Only one shop window was lighted, and he spent five minutes gazing at the display of cigarette packages, all of brands that were unknown to him.

He did not know that on this route, at this hour of the night, there was a forty-minute wait between streetcars. He spent the last ten minutes sitting alone in the dark. It had not been thought worthwhile to turn on the lights merely for his convenience before the streetcar started out on its journey back into the town.

No telegram from Cosson at the poste restante. He had checked to ascertain whether all telegrams so addressed were automatically delivered to the general post office.

The weather was more oppressive than it had been until now. The sky was overcast, heavy with a storm that threatened but had not yet broken. He had lunched on kidneys in Madeira, which had lain heavy on his stomach all afternoon.

He had noted that not far from the avenue in the town center was a district consisting almost entirely of cabarets and nightclubs. He had finally decided to go there that evening, and about ten o'clock he went into the largest of these establishments, the Cristal-Palace.

In a sense, he could justly claim that he had always lived alone, for even in Bugle—making his house calls, holding his office hours, sitting at the table surrounded by his family—he was always deep in his own thoughts. Not that these thoughts were of any particular significance: they were no more than disjointed reminiscences, responses to small incidents, sounds, changes of light, the hammering in Halkin's workshop, the children shouting in the school playground. . . . Admittedly it was a different kind of solitude he was experiencing now, and it sometimes made him feel uneasy, as if there were something shameful in it.

Here in the Cristal-Palace, for instance. The dance hall was vast and crowded with people. There were two bands alternating; according to which one was playing, the lighting changed from violet to pink. There were tables all around the dance floor and rows of little cubicles on either side.

"Excuse me, is this seat vacant?"

He was sitting alone at a table. He had a feeling that he was being watched. He was beginning to wish he had never come when all of a sudden he recognized a face in one of the cubicles, the face of the fat Flemish girl of the mussel episode. He looked away quickly, but not before he had caught a glimpse of a dim figure beside her, a naval officer in white summer uniform.

It was of no importance. . . . Nothing had happened between them. . . . She was hardly likely to accost him just in order to vent her ill humor on him again! . . . Nevertheless, frowning, he studiously averted his eyes. He heard a voice call out:

"Cricri!"

And then he heard it again.

In vain, he looked about him. It had been years since anyone had called him by that name. In Bugle, certainly, no one would have dared to address him thus, now that he was a doctor. It had been his nickname at the lycée, though no one quite knew why, perhaps because he was small, curt of speech, and nervous, jumpy as a cricket—*cricri* was what French children called a cricket.

The naval officer stood up, leaned across, and shouted: "Hi, Cricri!"

People were turning around to look at Bergelon, who by now had recognized his former schoolmate, Clarius, and had no choice but to go over to the cubicle, mumbling "Excuse me!" as he struggled through a stream of people who were returning to their tables from the dance floor.

Should he pretend not to recognize the fat girl? It was really up to her to decide. . . .

"Well, well, my dear old friend, Cricri! What on earth are you doing here? Take a seat. . . . Allow me to introduce you to a friend of mine, Mina. . . . I'll tell you all about it later. . . ."

They made room for him, and Clarius looked around for the waiter to ask him to bring another glass. For there was already a bottle of champagne on the table.

"Well?"

Well, nothing! What could Bergelon possibly say in answer to that? Not only was this meeting with Clarius totally unexpected, but he scarcely knew him, anyway. It was an odd sensation to find oneself being addressed so familiarly by someone whom one had not set eyes on for thirteen or fourteen years! Moreover, they had never been friends. His mother had never tired of repeating:

"I forbid you to play with that little guttersnipe, Clarius. . . ."

Clarius's parents were not legally married. It was even said that his mother had formerly been a prostitute.

As for Clarius himself, he was a hefty, somewhat ungainly little brute. He played the tough, was always getting into fights, and was suspended from the lycée at least once a term; in the end he was expelled once and for all.

Bergelon had seen him only one time after leaving school, wearing mechanic's overalls.

"I'll be damned if I ever imagined I'd run across you in Antwerp! Is your wife here as well? I did hear that you'd married the daughter of that man who sold heating appliances."

Clarius had grown up very broad and thickset. Had he been less muscular, he might almost have been described as fat.

"On vacation?"

He was one of the few local boys of whom Bergelon had completely lost sight. He had even forgotten his existence. All he could remember about him was that at about the age of twenty, Clarius had received a prison sentence. He also vaguely recalled having heard that he had joined the navy in Toulon.

"Well, old boy!"

He slapped Bergelon on the knee. Mina did not stir. She just sat there, mild and placid, as when she had eaten her steak and fries.

"Cheers! By the way, weren't you my father's doctor? Poor old fellow! He died last year of a heart attack. Oh, well, it's a marvelous way to go. . . ."

"Shh!" hissed the people next to them, because there was a performance in progress by a Spanish dancer who was accompanying herself with castanets, but Clarius was not to be silenced by such an interruption. He knew what was what! Little did he care that he was being glared at furiously by three or four rows of spectators.

"You really must come and pay me a visit on board. . . . I'm captain of my own ship now, you know . . . a Greek tanker. . . . It would take too long to explain. . . . Don't you live in Bugle any more?"

"No."

"Have you left for good?"

"Well . . ."

"Is it a woman? And while we are on that subject . . . Hang on! I'll see what can be arranged. . . . Mina!"

He got up and went to the back of the cubicle, taking his companion with him. He said something to her in an undertone. She nodded unenthusiastically and left the cubicle. Clarius returned to his seat, observed by the Spanish dancer, who gave him a dirty look every time a pirouette brought her face to face with him.

"She's a good sort . . . practical, you know . . . just the woman I need when I'm in Antwerp. . . . I should tell you, I put in here for three or four days about once a month. . . . Have you really made up your mind to leave Bugle?"

"More or less."

"What will you do? Stick to medicine?"

"I don't know."

Clarius was altogether too ebullient for Bergelon. He felt crushed by the force of his personality. Furthermore, Bergelon could not rid himself of the mistrust of the man engendered by the indoctrination his mother had given him when he was a child.

"What do they say about me in Bugle? At any rate, they can't complain of seeing too much of me. How many years is it now, since I got my master's certificate? Five years . . . Nothing doing in France . . . especially after that business in Toulon, when I was doing my military service aboard the *Duquesne*. . . . I roamed around the Mediterranean for a while. . . . The Greeks are no fools when it comes to shipping. . . . They have this dodge. . . . They buy up old ships that other countries won't touch because they're too expensive to insure . . . and then they operate them uninsured. . . . They've got fantastic seamen out there. . . . They work for peanuts and live on rice and potatoes soused in olive oil . . . plus red peppers!"

He leaned forward and peered across to the far end of the room, where Bergelon could see Mina in conversation with another woman. They seemed to be having quite a fierce argument. The woman seemed reluctant to go along with Mina's suggestions. Every now and then one or the other of them would glance toward the cubicle.

"To make a long story short, I got myself a berth on one of those old tubs. . . . Oil, Russian oil . . . Batum–Antwerp . . . Antwerp–Batum . . . Batum–Antwerp . . . It's always the same. Here, I always look up Mina, who has a nice little place of her own, and who is fastidiously clean. . . . In Russia, it depends. . . . As for my wife . . ."

"Are you married?"

It was an effort to address him by the familiar *tu*. Bergelon had always found it difficult to use that form of address with anyone.

"Married, with two children. Not divorced, but separated. My wife is in Barcelona. She's Spanish. When it dawned on us that we were incompatible, we parted the best of friends, and we still write to one another from time to time. . . . Look!"

From a thick wallet, stuffed with papers, he produced a photograph of a boy of about ten.

"That's my eldest! Believe it or not, he's at school with the Jesuits. Isn't that a riot? My wife runs a small dress shop. She manages to get by. . . ."

"Excuse me."

Mina and her friend came into the cubicle. Solemnly, Mina made the introductions:

"My friend, Marcelle."

Marcelle was thin and dark, a taller version of Edna.

"My friend, Captain Clarius . . . Monsieur . . ."

"Cricri!" interrupted Clarius. "Just call him that. . . . Waiter! Another glass . . . We won't order another bottle now—we'll open one on board. . . . It's a lot cheaper, being duty-free. . . . Guess what the finest champagne costs me on board. . . . Thirty francs! And vintage at that! As for you, ladies, if you feel so inclined, why not dance together? We two still have things to discuss. . . ."

They obeyed without protest. From time to time they put their heads together and whispered to one another, like the Salvation Army women on the streetcar.

"Joking aside . . . Maybe you'll tell me to mind my own business. . . . Are you in need of a job? . . . Have you done something foolish, is that it? An abortion?"

"No."

"No matter! Keep it to yourself, if that's what you'd prefer. But if, by any chance, you're looking for a cushy billet . . . Do you know Trebizond? No, of course, I'd forgotten, you've never strayed far from your own back yard, have you? A cigar? No? When I'm ashore I never stop smoking . . . because, on board, with five or six thousand tons of oil underfoot . . . Oh, by the way, what do you think of the girl? Not too bad, eh? She's yours! Yes, I mean it! . . . We're all going to get together on board my ship, like old friends. . . . What was I saying? Oh, yes . . . in principle, we're not supposed to put in anywhere en route. On the other hand, at times, when you're dealing with old ships, it's sometimes necessary for safety's sake to run for shelter, especially in the Black Sea. . . . And that's how I came to put in at Trebizond. . . ."

"In Turkey?" said Bergelon, intrigued in spite of himself.

"In Turkey as you say . . . a quaint little town, with a steep main street, and market stalls with sides of lamb roasting on spits, and a lot of strange fellows in white robes, looking as if they'd come straight out of the desert. . . . Just you wait and see . . . at least, you'll see if you decide to come. . . . One thing I can tell you: the old French doc who looked after all the best people had just died last time I put in there. . . . They were looking for a replacement. And now that they've got used to having a Frenchman . . ."

The two women rejoined them, awaiting further orders.

"Waiter! What do I owe you? Let me see the wine list."

He was determined to check the price. Having done so, he paid.

"Let's be going!"

And outside:

"You two go on ahead."

To Bergelon he said:

"It's not far. . . . There'll be plenty of time to have fun later. . . . But seriously, how would you like to settle in Trebizond? Because if you're interested, I'll sign you on board. We sail tomorrow, on the evening tide. . . ."

It was the name, more than anything else, that appealed to Bergelon. Trebizond . . . the steep main street . . . the grilled lamb . . . the camels . . . for he was sure there must be camels, although no mention had been made of them.

"Don't worry . . . Mina knows the way."

He meant the way to the dock where his ship was berthed. The two women walked on ahead, arm in arm. They looked like a couple of housewives returning home from the movies on a Saturday night. Other couples, other groups of people, were about, their footsteps ringing on the cobblestones.

"Before we get to the fun and games, I must show you my paintings. . . . Have you forgotten? Even as a little kid, I used to paint watercolors. . . . On board ship, where there's practically nothing to do for days on end, I took it up again.

"Halt!" he shouted, in a totally different voice.

They had reached the dock gates. He spoke a few words to the customs official, then handed him a cigar.

"Watch out for the ropes!"

They stepped over them. The dock was lit by arc lamps, so cruelly bright as to be almost unbearable.

"It's the third along . . . the *Theseus*. Can you still read the Greek alphabet? I can speak most languages a bit . . . or rather a mixture of all of them."

As if to prove it, he spoke in a language unknown to Bergelon to the seaman on guard at the foot of the gangway.

"Careful! . . . Take it slowly. . . . Follow me."

They had to step over various iron projections and climb an iron ladder, very slippery on account of the damp night air.

"Don't move. . . . I'll turn on the light."

In an instant they found themselves in a little stateroom, very clean and cozy, furnished with a red divan, a desk, several armchairs, and framed watercolors on the walls.

"Ahmed! Ahmed!"

A strapping young boy appeared from nowhere, rubbing the sleep out of his eyes.

"Put two bottles of champagne in the refrigerator. Bring us some pastries, and then make yourself scarce."

And to the two women:

"Make yourselves at home. . . . Mina, you know your way around, isn't that so? We'll be back in a minute."

A glance at Bergelon, inviting him to follow him into the cabin next door, Clarius's sleeping quarters.

"Look at this. To revert to Trebizond, this is a view of the coast during a storm. . . ."

Everything was in apple-pie order and very clean. The bed was already turned down, and on the pillow was a pair of silk pajamas embroidered with a green dragon. Clarius removed his jacket, and looking at himself in the mirror, smoothed down his hair, having first handed a sheaf of watercolors to his companion.

"Give me your honest opinion. They're not bad, are they? At the beginning I used to work from postcards, but lately I've branched out and started painting from nature. It's harder than you'd think. . . . Excuse me a moment. . . ."

He opened a door, revealing a dimly lit wheelhouse.

"There's just one thing I must ask you, and that is not to smoke. . . . One can't be too strict about that. . . . What do you think of my accommodations? This is where I spend nearly all my time . . . that little stateroom in there . . . my cabin . . . And then there's the chart-room, where I do most of my painting, because that's where the best light is. . . . No one to bother me. . . . At Batum I stock up with loads of caviar, which costs practically nothing. . . . As for girls, I always have stacks of fashion magazines from Paris, and there's nothing they wouldn't do to get them. In Antwerp I have Mina, and she doesn't cost me much. . . . As to how she makes a living . . ."

Still standing in front of the mirror, he gargled with pink mouthwash that smelled strongly of aniseed; then he went into the bathroom. There was the sound of running water, then his voice, shouting:

"By the way, is your mother still alive? Do make yourself at home, won't you? Loosen up a bit. . . . I can't offer you a pair of my pajamas; you'd swim in them. . . . Wait, though! Ahmed! Ahmed! Where the hell are you?"

Ahmed reappeared.

"Go and get a clean pair of pajamas and some slippers from Monsieur Tedesco's cabin . . . and be quick about it!"

And to Bergelon:

"Tedesco is my second-in-command . . . a Romanian. . . . I'll bet he's in some gambling den this very minute, losing every penny of his earnings, all he's saved in the last month on board. . . ."

He returned to the cabin, carrying a towel.

"And now that's enough serious talk for the present. Agreed? Let's go see what the girls have been up to."

He opened the door of the stateroom. The room had undergone a transformation. The two women had undressed in the men's absence and were wearing dressing gowns that, like Clarius's pajamas, came from China or Japan. The new girl was still not feeling quite at ease; to avoid showing her embarrassment she had stretched out on the divan.

On the table were two bottles of champagne in ice buckets and several florid boxes containing exotic sweets, such as Turkish delight and odd-shaped cookies.

"What do you mean by leaving all these lights blazing?"

Clarius switched off half of them, then later turned them all off, except one dim bulb above the divan. He opened a little door in the paneling, pressed a switch, and a phonograph record started to play.

He did all this composedly, reminding Bergelon a little of Germaine going about her ritual tasks on a Sunday morning, getting the children dressed, preparing a picnic for the afternoon outing.

"Warm enough?" he inquired of Mina's friend, who

was huddled in the shadows on the divan, looking a little scared.

He turned to Bergelon and winked.

"Anyone care for a drink? What have we here? Mumm Cordon Rouge '29 . . . Yes, what is it, Ahmed?"

"I couldn't find any pajamas."

"Never mind. He'll just have to do without!"

He uncorked one of the bottles and filled the glasses.

"Wake me at eight, Ahmed. I have an urgent appointment with the harbormaster at nine. . . . Lay out my serge suit. . . . Understood? Off you go, then."

And finally, in gruff, jovial tones:

"End of playtime, children! We have more serious matters to attend to. By the way, what's your name? . . . Marcelle? Well, then, Marcelle, if you want any champagne, show us your tits. . . . Come on, closer . . . good . . . you'll do. . . . And your pussy? God save us! It's as black as hell! Everything to your taste, Cricri? Cheers! Let's drink to . . . to Trebizond. Well, is it yes?"

"It's . . ."

"It's yes! And now, leave us in peace. . . . Look after him, will you, Marcelle?"

The appalling thing was that Bergelon had had nothing to drink! He was still agonizingly sober!

And he lacked the courage to make his escape.

Chapter Ten

*T*he cabin belonged to one of the officers—the second, was it, or the third? He could not remember. Clarius had told him some story about this cabin. What was it, now? Anyway, why should it matter? Everything was white, smooth, and glowing, with here and there a warm glint of brass; the noises that had penetrated Bergelon's consciousness some time before, while he was still in a deep sleep, continued to pervade everything with their metallic clanging. The hammering on sheet metal of Halkin's blacksmiths were mere tinklings compared with the fearsome clashing of iron which broke out every few seconds, reverberating throughout the dock area, sometimes near at hand, sometimes farther off, occasionally on the ship itself, causing every rivet to vibrate until it seemed that the whole world was filled with the clanging of massive steel. And yet, the effect of all this racket was somehow reassuring—it gave one a feeling of peace, of power safely and wholesomely deployed. There was no sense of evil. Even the strident shrilling of whistles was not an aggressive sound.

The cabin was narrow. Everything was within reach. Everything was gleaming. Opening a door, Bergelon discovered a doll-sized bathroom, with a shower that sent out a spray of warm water at the turn of a tap. He had looked at his watch. It was ten o'clock. Standing in the bathtub with water streaming down on him—this water had a curious, metallic smell, no doubt from having been stored in the ballast tanks—he could see through the porthole another shimmering expanse of water and a sailor pushing a boat out with an oar. He stood waiting for a few seconds, and then he frowned. At first he thought that it was only the boat that was moving. Then it struck him as odd that although it was indeed moving, it still remained in view through the porthole. At last, light dawned: the ship, also, was on the move!

He lost no time in drying himself, scrambling into his clothes, and rushing out on deck. Endeavoring to get his bearings, he found that the dock was no longer where it had been. Close alongside was another ship, towering above him like a wall, with scarcely a lick of paint on her hull; and there was a tiny tug at the front of the tanker, towing it through a tide gate. They were still in the harbor, but they had crossed to the other side while he was asleep. Two sailors were unrolling cable from a winch, while several others were paying it out by hand.

He felt a sudden stab of anguish. He climbed the nearest iron ladder and asked the first man he saw:

"Where's the captain?"

"He's just come back on board. He must be in his stateroom with the representative of Veritas."

From the wheelhouse he looked through the porthole into the stateroom. Everything was in perfect order, and the mahogany furniture and paneling gleamed. There were a bottle of whisky and glasses on the table, at which Clarius, wearing his navy blue uniform with its gold-braided cuffs and cap, was talking to a civilian whose back was toward Bergelon.

Clarius, catching sight of the doctor, stood up, murmured something to his companion, and came into the wheelhouse, shutting the door behind him.

"I've decided to put to sea on this tide."

Then, realizing that he had not said good morning, he shook his friend's hand:

"O.K.?"

And he went on:

"That means we'll be able to navigate the Scheldt on the evening tide. . . . We'll cast anchor in mid-channel."

He looked surprisingly cool, pink-cheeked and fresh. All he needed, it seemed, was a shower to restore him to his normal self. Although he had been up since eight, rushing hither and thither from one office to another, he showed no sign of the night's debauchery except perhaps a slight puffiness about the eyelids.

He made no further allusion to it. It was over, forgotten. He had work to do. He had business to discuss with the representative of Veritas.

"By the way, if anyone asks, I have put you on the roster as the company agent. You'd better nip into town and get some things. If we had been putting in at Malta, you'd have found clothes cheaper there than anywhere else, but we won't be stopping there this trip. Your best course would be to go and see a Chinese fellow I know. I'll write down his address for you. He has ready-to-wear linen suits in stock. If they're not a perfect fit, he'll do any necessary alterations within the hour. So long as you're back on board by two o'clock. The sentry on duty will show you where we're berthed."

He stopped a passing sailor.

"Would you show this gentleman ashore?"

Then:

"See you later!"

Bergelon had to climb over the rail and then down the side of the ship by a rope ladder. A few minutes later, he was standing, looking bewildered, at the foot of some stone steps covered in green slime. He did not know his way about the docks, but walked on until he reached an embankment in an area that he did not recognize.

At this point, in spite of his reluctance to part with money, he decided to take a taxi.

"General post office."

He was in the grip of a strange sort of agitation, subtle and indefinable, as if he had just escaped some danger that had threatened him.

"Bergelon . . . spelled as it's pronounced," he murmured, poking his head through the window of the poste restante counter.

And while a clerk in a gray apron was flipping through a pile of letters, he could not stop his hands from shaking.

"A telegram . . . There's a surcharge of one franc seventy-five to pay."

In little cubicles against the wall people were drafting telegrams and filling in forms. It was a place full of shadows. He opened his telegram.

WILL BE IN PARIS AFTERNOON EIGHTEENTH BEFORE LEAVING COUNTRY FOR GOOD STOP / CAN BE CONTACTED AT RESTAURANT DAUMAL NEAR GARE DU NORD / COSSON

The place of origin was not Paris, but Bugle. He looked about him for a calendar and saw that today was the seventeenth. Before doing anything else he went into a café for a glass of beer. He asked for some writing materials. But he still had plenty of time. He walked to the station, still so uncontrollably agitated that his knees shook.

"There's the *Etoile du Nord* leaving in half an hour."

It was almost as if he stood in dread of being detained by some mysterious, unknown authority. A quarter of an hour before the train was due to leave, he was already installed in a second-class car. He had not written to Clarius. He had not gone back to the Oude Antwerp to take leave of his landlady, collect his suitcase, and pay his bill.

So precipitate had been his flight that he arrived in Paris much too soon, that same day while the sun was still high in the sky. Although there were twenty-four hours yet to go, he nevertheless made inquiries about the Restaurant Daumal, fearing that without the full address he might be unable to locate it.

But he had no difficulty finding it, an undistinguished restaurant directly opposite the station.

Struggle against it as he might, he was still feverish, anxious as if he had just escaped—for the time being—from some danger. Mechanically, he checked to see that he still had his wallet, fearing that he might have dropped it or had it stolen in the crowded station.

He went to see a movie but paid scant attention to it. When he came out it took him a few seconds to realize that he was in Paris. The theater was on Boulevard Magenta, where he had never been before.

He slept badly, imagining that he could still hear the clamor of the docks, giants striking iron with colossal hammer blows; every now and then he would wake with a start, with the feeling that his bed was tilting, having broken from its moorings, and that . . .

"Do you know anyone named Jean Cosson?"

"Who's he?"

"He arranged to meet me here. I presume he's one of your customers."

"We have so many! What does he look like?"

"Tall and thin . . . youngish, wears his hair rather long . . ."

"I don't see . . ."

At the Restaurant Daumal he had lunch, followed by coffee and a glass of fine champagne. He had chosen a table near the window so he could see everyone coming in. He was growing impatient. He thought of the tanker, far out in the North Sea, which was bathed in brilliant light and stretched as far as the eye could see.

Then suddenly, at about five minutes to five, a taxi drew up at the entrance. Cosson got out; he lifted out a suitcase and a number of oddly shaped parcels, one by one. As he stood on the sidewalk paying the fare he was surrounded by packages.

Only then did he turn around. Recognizing Bergelon through the glass, he came inside, laden at first with three of the parcels.

"Just a minute."

He went out to fetch the others, mopped his forehead, and summoned the waitress.

"A beer, and be quick about it!"

He was drenched in perspiration. His face was flushed, and his eyes were more feverishly bright than ever.

"Phew! My train leaves in less than an hour! I was afraid you might not come."

He drank his beer in a single gulp, his Adam's apple bobbing up and down as he struggled to get his breath.

"Another beer?" suggested Bergelon.

He hesitated.

"Yes. . . . No. . . . It will only make me sweat even

more. . . . I got here at nine this morning, and I've been shopping ever since. Luckily I found a second-hand place where they had most of the things I needed."

He had spoken without so much as a glance at the doctor. Now he looked at him with a slight smile, as if across a great gulf.

"What did you think when you got my telegram?"

He mopped his face again. His parcels were blocking the entrance, so, glad of an excuse to keep on the move, he brought them over to the table.

"You haven't asked me where I'm going."

He looked a little crazy, his eyes flashing with exultation and pride. He was longing to pour it all out. He fumbled in his wallet and took out a crumpled newspaper clipping.

"There! Read that. . . ."

Leaning back in his chair, he felt in his bulging pockets for cigarettes and matches, then called to the waitress:

"A brandy and water . . . What will you have, doctor?"

"Nothing more, thanks," replied Bergelon, engrossed in his reading.

It had arrived one morning at about eleven o'clock. The window of the room over the shoemaker's shop was open. All the windows on Rue des Minimes were open, and he could hear every sound from the neighboring houses—the monotonous wailing of a baby and, somewhere or other, the thump of a flatiron on a padded ironing board.

Cécile, in her dressing gown, was writing at the table, which was still littered with the breakfast things: coffee pot, milk jug, empty cups, an open bowl of sugar covered with flies. The bed was unmade. There was listlessness and inertia in the air. Cosson, in his shirt sleeves and bedroom slippers, had tilted back his chair to rest his feet on the window sill; he was reading a newspaper, of which the sun—like a powerful reading lamp—illuminated one side.

"What did I tell you to ask for?"

It was the voice of the woman who lived next door. Her coarse, shrill voice could be heard every morning above the stoking of the range and all the other household noises.

"Beefsteak," replied the voice of a little girl.

"Of course, beefsteak. But how much?"

"I forget."

"You don't know how much meat you asked for? Very well! I'll tell you again! It's the same every day. I said a quarter of a kilo."

"A quarter of a kilo," repeated the child, whom Cosson knew to be a fat, round-faced brat.

"In that case, why have you brought back three hundred and fifty grams? Do you really imagine that I can afford three hundred and fifty grams of meat? Eh? Answer me! Do you think that out of the thirty-five francs your father earns, when he lets me have the money, I can pay . . ."

She had a lot more to say on the subject, in the same strident tones.

"Will you please stop looking at me like that, and stop scratching your nose, do you hear me?"

Unable to contain herself any longer, she seized her daughter by the shoulders and shook her, and then there were floods of tears.

JOURNAL OF A TOUR OF AFRICA

Turning to the second page of the newspaper, Cosson began reading an article, some of which he was unable to take in on account of the woman next door. The sun was pouring down not only on the printed page but also on his knees, warming them pleasantly.

Yesterday, quite by chance, we came upon a most picturesque sight. Our little caravan was traveling along a barely distinguishable trail, which sloped upward through even more sparse vegetation. Suddenly our driver's arm shot out, and he pointed to a cloud of dust, ablaze in the sunlight. A few minutes later, we caught up with the last thing we were expecting to see, an ancient truck of a kind seldom found in Europe any longer. It was being driven by two Arab-type Negroes, one of them wearing an old pith helmet, and the other a cap of the sort worn by those louts one sees at home round about the Bastille.

The strangest thing about this truck was that it was a sort of traveling shop, loaded with the kind of goods sold by peddlers in remote country districts in France. It was fitted with racks and shelves, stacked with merchandise of every sort—a most incongruous assortment, including such surprising items as condensed milk, suspenders, and some quite indescribable purple socks.

As we had been driving for hours with not so much as a village in sight, we wondered where this mobile shop could possibly be bound for, and our interpreter got out and spoke to the two men. One of them spoke a kind of pidgin French.

"Kibi!" he said, pointing to the wilderness ahead of us. . . . "Gold mines . . . Lots people . . . Come from everywhere . . ."

And so it was that in the foothills of the Upper Volta we found the most picturesque of gold mines.

"The article goes on here," said Cosson, turning over the page and refolding the paper.

"You'll be in a fine way when I have to go into the hospital," continued the shrew, who was scouring saucepans with sand, thus producing a monotonous grinding sound.

"And if things go on like this, I very likely will land up in the hospital! A woman who is eight months pregnant shouldn't have to do all her own housework, including humping pails of water and scuttles full of coal up the stairs, especially with a good-for-nothing daughter like you! Do you know what your father would do, if I was to die? He'd put you into the care of the local authorities! That's what he would do!"

The little girl burst into tears, crying not because she understood but because the words "care of the local authorities" had come to be a nightmare to her; she had only to hear them spoken to dissolve in tears.

"That's all I want . . . Tears, is it now? A fat lot of help to me that is. . . . I've been asking myself for days what it is I've done to displease the good Lord. . . . Would you please stop wiping your face with those filthy hands of yours? . . . If you don't do as you're told, I'll give you a good slap!"

Cosson was still reading.

What an amazing thing, to find a gold mine—or rather gold deposits—that have not already been exploited by a commercial company. As a rule, where there is gold, there are Englishmen. Here there is not a single one, in spite of the fact that we are so close to the border of a British protectorate.

We were told that the existence of these deposits has been known for a long time and that in all probability they are the ones mentioned in *The Voyages of Captain Singleton*, when the companions of the Captain-to-be spent weeks, before reaching the Atlantic, panning for gold in an upland river bed.

For a short period, the deposits were owned by a consortium, but apparently the returns were insufficient to cover the costs.

At first, after it was abandoned, only a few Negroes were attracted there. Then suddenly there was a gold rush comparable, though on a smaller scale, to that which occurred in the United States in the last century. Several whole villages of blacks converged on the region, equipped only with primitive sieves.

There are now almost two thousand people of all races, toiling from morning to night under the blazing sun, standing up to their ankles in the river.

It is a strange sight to see clumps of mud huts side by side with wooden shacks with corrugated iron roofs, and Negroes almost naked—sometimes, indeed, completely naked—working alongside Arabs dressed in European clothes. Some of the natives wear an old dinner jacket or simply an old dress shirt, the front of which had once been starched.

Traders of all sorts have been attracted to the region. One, a Greek, buys the gold dust after weighing it on a queer-looking pair of scales. Another, from Portugal, has erected a vast warehouse of wooden planks, from which he sells everything under the sun, including old phonograph records. These are played all day long, and nothing could be more incongruous, in this wild, remote countryside, than to hear Viennese waltzes, operatic arias, and military marches.

I have inquired as to the profits made by all this industry, and I was told that by panning assiduously it is possible to earn about twelve francs a day.

The locals can live on two francs a day, and are therefore left with a profit of ten francs, but most of this money goes into the pocket of the man who sells records, to the bar, and to peddlers like the two we met, who bring in quantities of trash from the coast.

It should be mentioned that among this mob of colored men we encountered, not without some sense of shame, three white men who were working like blacks and squabbling with them over territory.

"Are you finished with it?" asked Cosson, greedily snatching back his precious paper.

"Believe it or not, just as I was coming to the end of that article, Cécile looked up from her writing and asked:

" 'Are there two *p*'s in "occupy"?'

"Suddenly I couldn't stand another minute of it. I was furiously angry. The little girl next door was yelling her head off, and her mother was shouting even louder. And one of my knees was blistered with sunburn.

" 'Who are you writing to?' I asked her.

" 'You know perfectly well.'

"You bet I did! Who else would she be writing to but her boyfriend in Poissy? Mind you, I'm not saying that it was any fault of hers that I was sick of everything. It was the whole atmosphere: the streets, the kid yelling, the room all messy, and me feeling as limp as a rag, as I always do in the morning when I've had too much to drink the night before.

" 'I forbid you to write to him.'

" 'But, Jean . . .'

" 'Never mind the "Jean," do you hear! Do as I tell you! And what's more, I've had just about enough . . .'

" 'What's the matter with you?'

" 'The matter with me? I'm fed up! Damn well fed up!'

"I was shouting at the top of my voice. And the more she looked at me in that placid, indulgent way of hers, the more I wanted to hit her . . . and I did hit her. . . . I provoked her to such an extent that she stood up and made for the door, saying:

" 'I'll come back when you're in a more reasonable frame of mind.'

" 'Come here!'

" 'No!'

" 'Come here!'

"Because, you see, she was still in her dressing gown, so I knew she had in mind seeking refuge with one of the neighbors.

"I gave her a beating such as I'd never given anyone before. Then I got dressed, and all the while she just lay there on the bed, looking at me, not crying, just stunned. I picked up my newspaper and left. When I got back to my own place and went into the bedroom and saw the crib and . . .

"Oh, what the hell! I sobbed like a child. I think I must have been howling, like a dog howling at the moon, because the pork butcher came all the way upstairs and called through the door to ask if there was anything he could do for me. . . .

"Next day, I asked him to make me an offer for everything in the apartment. . . .

"I went to see my mother and told her I was going away for good.

"The butcher gave me a thousand francs. Mind you, more than half the stuff was bought on installments, and not paid for, but what the hell!

"I made inquiries about how to get out to Africa. First you have to get to Grand Bassam. It's too expensive by passenger steamer, and besides, there isn't one sailing from Bordeaux for a week, but I've found a cargo boat that takes an occasional passenger for the price of his food. It sails tomorrow morning from Boulogne."

Time passed. His hand was shaking. The hands of the clock over the entrance of the Gare du Nord jerked forward minute by minute.

Then, starkly, Jean Cosson asked:

"And you?"

This "and you?" so unforced yet so eloquent, sent the

blood rushing to Bergelon's head. It was no ordinary question. It implied much more than could be said in the course of a long conversation.

How was it to be interpreted?

"And you? What's been happening to you?"

No! That was not it. There was a great deal more to it than that.

"Where do you stand?"

Better.

"What is your solution?"

That was more like it!

"You do understand, don't you, doctor? I'm not going out there in the hope of making my fortune, nor to live like a member of the master race. . . . If you could see what's in these parcels, you'd realize . . . Tropical equipment, new, costs a lot of money . . . but I remembered this second-hand place in Montmartre, where they had a whole lot of tropical kit in the window. . . .

"That's where I bought this chest . . . and an old pith helmet . . . and some linen suits, several sizes too big. . . . I wanted to buy a gun. They had them in stock, but you have to have a special license. . . ."

He was so impatient to be gone that he could hardly breathe.

"I don't know why it was I felt so sure you'd come. . . . I suggested meeting you here because I couldn't think of the name of any other restaurant. This is where we came for dinner on our honeymoon."

He was on the verge of tears.

"Tell me the truth. . . . Her life could have been saved, couldn't it? And the baby's too?"

Bergelon blinked, but did not reply.

"There are times when I ask myself whether it isn't perhaps all for the best. Yes, I sometimes wonder whether I would have stuck it out to the end. . . ."

His eyes bored into the little doctor's face. They seemed to be saying:

"Like you, for instance!"

He rattled on, switching from one idea to another, with an occasional anxious glance at the electric clock.

"Cécile was at the station. . . . I don't know how she knew I was leaving town. . . . She wanted to give me a little money. She swore to me that she bears me no grudge, and that if I should ever need her . . . As far as my wife is concerned, I don't know how long our marriage would have lasted. . . ."

His restless glance was never still. His eyes moved from someone going past the table to his glass, from the waitress to Bergelon.

"Tell me about yourself. What are you going to do?"

Behind those words was much that he would not or dared not say.

"You wouldn't? . . ."

No! He turned his head away. Had he been going to say:

"You wouldn't come with me, would you?"

Then, finally taking a firm grip on his feelings, he joked, not without a hint of a swagger:

"Do you realize that I could have killed you? At one stage, when I ceased to care what became of me, it was an obsession with me. Please note that it never occurred to me to kill your colleague Mandalin. I don't know why . . . perhaps because he was a total stranger to me. No, you were the one! And when I mentioned a bomb, I really was serious. I had even gone so far as to set aside an empty can, a can that had contained peas. It must still be there under Cécile's bed. Out there, there will soon be another white man among the blacks. Apparently the sun is so fierce—mind you, I read this in a novel, so it may not be true—so fierce that a man on a train was struck blind by its reflection off one of the rails on the track. . . . You can't wear rubber soles because they melt. . . . The real joke is that my mother is greatly relieved! Guess what she said to me—that she'd rather see me dead than disgraced, and that she prayed to God day and night that . . ."

He broke off in mid-sentence, suddenly overcome with emotion. He turned toward the window to hide his feelings.

"When I got on the train in Bugle . . ."

He was too choked to be able to go on. He needed a drink, but his glass was empty. There was a mirror on the wall opposite. Looking at his reflection, he twisted his lips into a bitter smile, which gradually turned into an angry scowl.

"They make me sick, all of them!" he snapped.

He turned slowly to look Bergelon full in the face. Bergelon felt a sense of shame. Memories of the war came into his mind, memories passed on by an older generation.

"That's what! I'm enlisting! What about you?"

For that was exactly the tone adopted by Cosson a moment ago, when he had asked:

"And you?"

And now, as he looked at the doctor with a quizzical expression, there was the same question, unspoken this time, in Cosson's eyes.

And what about him? What *did* he propose to do?

Cosson had spoken out! Cosson had committed himself! Cosson was going to see it through to the end!

He was apprehensive, that much was obvious from the fact that he ordered another brandy and water to keep his courage up, from his anxious expression as he glanced at the clock every few seconds.

Still twenty minutes to go. Twenty minutes to wait,

then he would be on the train. He would arrive in Boulogne. He would hurry across the dock to the cargo ship. . . .

By then he would be very close to his goal!

A clear picture formed in Bergelon's head. He was gliding slowly through the water and looking out through a porthole, when there in the midst of an empty sea was a boat, seemingly motionless, with a tiny man, rowing. . . .

For him, that had been the moment of departure. . . . Cosson's journey, however, had already begun, and he could think of nothing to say to him. He simply looked at him with an expression of mingled fear, respect, and shame.

"Believe it or not, the other day your daughter caught sight of me in the street, and she took to her heels and fled as if she had seen the devil. When she reached your front door, she rattled the mailbox, and banged the door with her fists. She was in such a fearful state that I deliberately kept out of sight until your wife came to the door and let her in. . . ."

Bergelon could see it all as distinctly as if he had been present. Never before, not even when she was actually there in front of him, had he seen Annie's pale face so clearly.

"Check, please."

"Allow me. This is on me."

"No!"

"I must insist."

Bergelon was determined to pay for the drinks. Hastily he took a thousand-franc note from his wallet. He was struck by a sudden thought: Was it not the least he could do, to . . . ?

He hesitated. Cosson was looking elsewhere.

He still had nearly four thousand francs. . . . But it would be so mortifying! If he were to offer them to Cosson, it would be an admission that he was throwing in the towel.

"Are you going back to Antwerp?"

"I haven't made up my mind yet."

It was time to go. Humbly, Bergelon loaded himself up with half the parcels, but Cosson insisted on carrying the heaviest ones.

"Would you believe it, I couldn't find anyone able to advise me about panning equipment. In the end, I bought several wire mesh sieves of different gauges."

They stopped to let a stream of buses and taxis go by. In a few minutes Bergelon would be returning alone between the studs that marked the pedestrian crossing.

He knew that his companion was disillusioned, that he had nursed a faint hope . . .

"I think it's platform eight we want."

They made their way through the gray haze of dust in the station, bumping into suitcases and people in a hurry. What should he have said? Was he imagining it, or was Cosson hoping right up to the very last minute that something would happen to prevent him from going?

He looked even taller, thinner, bonier than usual.

"Here's the third class," he said, as Cosson peered at the cars.

Then, without bitterness, but with a strange sort of irony:

"Out there, I'll be worse off than a fourth-class passenger! By the way, if I should need to write to you . . ."

He had hesitated before asking the question, realizing that there was no possible answer

"Poste restante Paris will find me "

"Which P.O. box?"

He had to think of a number

"Forty-two."

The third-class cars were all full. Cosson's luggage was piled up right at the end of the corridor. Cosson himself, squeezed between a soldier and a young woman, was standing at the window.

"If you should decide to return to Bugle . . ." he began.

He retreated a step or two, ostensibly to make way for someone who wanted to get past. By the time he was back at the window he had decided to drop the subject of Bugle.

"These good people have no idea . . ." he murmured, leaning out.

The station guards were beginning to slam the doors of the train. Bergelon stood stock still. Next to him, a woman was waving a handkerchief and calling out to her daughter:

"Come now, there's no need to cry! You know it only upsets him. . . ."

He was not looking at them. He was watching Cosson. Cosson had a two days' growth of beard, his hair was longer than ever, his complexion sickly, and his eyes rimmed with red. He was laughing.

"I'm thinking of all those blacks!" he shouted.

He was determined to keep his end up to the last, but it seemed as if the train would never get started. Bergelon, too, was growing impatient. If this went on much longer, he would be casting dirty looks at the engine:

"Come on, move!"

Just at that moment steam began pouring not only from the engine but from all the brake valves as well, and the train jerked into motion. Cosson wanted to turn away but lacked the courage to do so. Instead, he waved his hand in front of his face.

"Do stop crying, you foolish girl!" the woman exhorted her daughter. "Can't you at least wait until you're out of his sight!"

Suddenly Bergelon found himself standing alone on an empty platform. He made a dash for the exit. For a second or two he was unable to lay his hands on his platform ticket. He fumbled in all his pockets.

In the end the ticket fell out of his handkerchief, and he bent down to pick it up.

Chapter Eleven

One ham, one! One cassoulet . . . Two fried eggs . .
One Port-Salut."

It was not a proper restaurant car, but a buffet car,
considerably less exclusive, although the pale-green paint
on the steel walls showed some effort to make it look
cheerful. However, the paint was already dirty. Even
with no breadcrumbs or wine stains on the embossed
paper tablecloths, the car would still have looked and
smelled overcrowded and neglected, the sort of place
where rubbish of all sorts is carelessly dropped on the
floor and graffiti written on the walls.

In the middle was a bar, surrounded by men who all
seemed to be talking at once, such was the volume of
noise produced by a comparatively small number of people. There were two soldiers, wearing the khaki uniforms,

puttees, and black caps of a colonial regiment. Another, looking uncomfortable in a blue civilian suit, was probably returning home on leave for the first time.

The air was thick with the smell of stale tobacco smoke and simmering cassoulet. Tucked away in a little cubicle a thin youth in a filthy apron could be seen, with his hair falling over his face, cooking the orders on a little gas ring.

The whole place was bathed in sunshine—sunshine in motion—intersected from time to time by thin telegraph poles or poplar trees; blotched with cool patches of shade each time the train swung around a corner, darkening the windows on one side as the light moved across to the other.

"Was I afraid to speak my mind? Eh, Frédéric?" He talked and talked. He had theories about this and theories about that, as if he thought he could change the world singlehanded.

The man who was speaking looked repulsive from the back, having a thick, coarse, purplish-red neck. He was eating with his fat legs wide apart, obstructing the waiter's path. He had a very loud voice and rolled his r's with the distinctive accent of central France. A cattle merchant or a wholesale butcher, probably.

It was the kind of talk commonly to be heard at election time, and, indeed, Bergelon had just seen a headline in a discarded newspaper, referring to the recent local elections in Moulins. Moulins was not far from Bugle. The two places shared a common district council.

"And so I came right out with it, I didn't pull any punches—if you don't believe me, ask Frédéric—I said to him: 'If you're so smart, how did you manage to get yourself cuckolded?' "

He slapped himself resoundingly on the thigh, then thumped his companions on the back, bellowing:

"Well, what do you think of that? I wasn't afraid to speak my mind!"

Two tables away sat a man between thirty-five and forty years of age, a slender, well-dressed, well-mannered person, probably a lawyer, a notary, or an examining magistrate, wearing a stiff collar and dark tie, with manicured hands, and with the thin ribbon of the Légion d'Honneur slotted through the lapel of his formal suit. In front of him, next to his plate of fried eggs, was a pile of documents that he had taken out of his briefcase. A faint smile played about his lips, ironic, no doubt, and expressive of an overwhelming sense of superiority. Judging Bergelon to be his social equal, he could not resist directing this smile at him, at the same time stroking his upper lip.

From time to time passengers passing along the corridor would pause to look in at the people eating. That morning all the men were wearing a flower in their buttonhole, a flower made of some furry material, an edelweiss.

It was Sunday. The Sunday devoted to the charity for the relief of tuberculosis; the flower chosen as a symbol was the mountain edelweiss. Girls acting as volunteers were selling them all over France. Children and teenagers, wearing armbands, were standing on street corners everywhere rattling their collecting boxes to attract passers-by.

The train was passing through undulating scenery, with fields sloping down to narrow streams. There were white cows dotted about, their heads bent and all turned in the same direction as they chewed the gleaming grass.

Suddenly Bergelon felt a stab of anguish. He was seized with giddiness. How far was it to Bugle? A hundred and fifty kilometers, a hundred? And yet he felt himself in the grip of irrational panic, as if something might still happen to prevent his reaching home.

White walls . . . enclosed gardens, trellises, vegetable plots . . . Sometimes as they approached a station an entire village would come into view, with youths in their navy or black Sunday suits, girls in white, pink, and pale blue, and men stumbling out of the inn, their white collars and shirtfronts contrasting sharply with their brick-red faces and wrinkled brown necks.

At one point a choir was walking in procession down a slope, with a banner in front. Elsewhere could be seen a merry-go-round and a shooting gallery, but it was early in the day and the fairground was deserted, except for two children sitting on the horses of the merry-go-round, which was rotating unaccompanied by music.

Meadows, fields, châteaux, glimpsed briefly between great clumps of trees, or cars coming into view around the bends of purple roads.

"You can take it from me—and I'm a pretty shrewd judge in these matters—that he'll lose a hundred votes on the second count, and Martin will win the seat. . . . They're a couple of bums, the pair of them, but at least Martin . . ."

Bergelon was standing in the corridor beside an open window, his hair blown about by the breeze, when he saw the soccer field, with its gray, wooden fence, its scattered players and rows of spectators, some standing, others sitting on the grass. And there was the last level crossing, the gasworks, the streets with their overhanging embankments . . .

He knew that today was not only Relief of Tuberculosis Sunday but also the day of pilgrimage to Notre-Dame d'Herbemont.

Where had he been the previous Sunday? At Riva-Bella. He could still picture himself on his balcony, watching the crowds from the nearby countryside pouring out of the local railroad station into the misty drizzle that enveloped the resort.

Only a week since then? And the Sunday before that? The Sunday before he had still been in Bugle, and he and all his family had picnicked in the Méran woods.

And yet, looking back, it seemed as if he had traveled much farther afield than Riva-Bella, Antwerp, and Paris. There had also been Trebizond, which had been very real to him in its way, with its narrow streets, its open-fronted shops with lamb roasting on spits, and camels coming in from the desert.

And then there was that other desert, he could not remember its name, a plateau scorched by the sun, with a river where two thousand Negroes padded in sand and mud, its shacks and mud huts, and the warehouse with its blaring phonograph, owned by a Portuguese who sold a little of everything, including records.

He was seized with a sudden urge to take flight! But here he was, already stepping down onto the concrete station platform, in the familiar shade, walking past the bench where he had so often sat waiting for his train, and handing in his ticket.

The square was almost empty. The atmosphere was so heavy that one could almost have sliced through it with a knife. It was Sunday. He was in Bugle. But he was not yet in his own parish, and, in spite of himself, he quickened his step, crossed the bridge, and walked to the end of one street and then another, the only living soul to be seen striding along the sun-baked sidewalks.

He knew—it was unthinkable that it should not be so—that the whole family, Germaine, Annie, and Mile, would be in Herbemont. The flavor of Herbemont was in his mouth, that distinctive flavor peculiar to places of pilgrimage. Every year, as far back as he could remember, the weather had been the same: hot, heavy, and humid, the air very still. In the late afternoon, just as they were within sight of the town, the storm that had been threatening all day would break in a torrential cloudburst.

They would set out in the morning, laden with provisions, straight after the ten o'clock Mass. This year Mile, as a Boy Scout, would be selling badges somewhere along the route.

At the bottom of the slope, near the Loire, hundreds of cars were parked, most of them unfamiliar, having come from the remote countryside. There were blankets laid out and, here and there, small trucks with chairs inside.

Tents had been erected, some selling rosaries and medallions, others soft drinks and lukewarm beer.

The route was narrow, stony, and very straight. It was hemmed in by hedges and was ordinarily very dull, but today hung with banners.

Every hundred yards or so were poles supporting glass cases containing groups of plaster figures, representing the stations of the cross. Flowers were piled up around them. There were hundreds of kneeling women, their lips moving in prayer and their fingers telling their rosary beads.

Annie was always the first to flag. She would keep them standing in the blazing sun, surrounded by a haze of dust that had a distinctive processional smell, stirred up by the feet of the passing crowds.

When at last they reached the chapel at the top of the hill, it was always a struggle to find a patch of grass under a tree where they could spread out their picnic.

He went past the Portals' house, but, it being Sunday, the carriage gates were shut. He passed other houses known well to him, quickened his pace, turned onto his own street, and was in sight of his own house. The shutters were closed, as were all the others along the street, which was as empty as a canal lock. He began to run; reaching his own doorstep, he put his hand in his pocket, only to discover that he did not have his key.

He rang the bell. There was just a chance that Monsieur Charles might be in. The bell echoed through the empty house. He looked through the keyhole and saw the dark hall and the glass door leading to the kitchen beyond.

There was only one way to get in, which he had often used as a child, and that was to call on Madame Pholien, whose back-garden wall, at one point, adjoined the Bergelons' for a yard or so. He could climb onto a chair and jump over, knowing that he would always find the kitchen door open. But as it turned out, Madame Pholien was herself at Herbemont! He looked through the keyhole, as he had done at his own front door, and all he could see was a marmalade-colored cat licking its haunches on the mat.

It was four o'clock. Germaine and the children would not be back before half past six. He began walking. The scruffy little bar opposite the movie theater was also deserted. He did not go in. Instead, he turned the corner and found himself on Rue des Minimes, where a few groups of people, mostly elderly, were sitting out on the sidewalk. An ice cream vendor, pushing his white cart, stopped from time to time and blew his little trumpet. The same man had been pushing the same cart when Bergelon was a child. He was Italian. The sides of his cart were decorated with painted scenes, one of which portrayed Mount Vesuvius in eruption.

Bergelon looked up and saw that the second-floor window above the shoemaker's was open. The shop below was shut. The front door of the living quarters was always left open.

He went in and began climbing the stairs, which smelled of poverty. For a moment or two he hesitated, standing on the mat outside Cécile's door. She must have heard him coming upstairs. He knocked.

"Who's there?"

Even as she spoke, she came to the door and opened it, her hand covered with soapsuds.

"Oh, it's you," she said, showing little surprise, though she had obviously not been expecting him. "Come in. And shut the door—otherwise it's so drafty."

Indeed, the window was on the point of slamming shut as he came in.

"If it's Jean you've come to see, he's not here any more."

It was Sunday for her, too. That is to say, it was different from other days. She was wearing nothing but a slip. She had not done her hair all day, and it was hanging down to her shoulders.

She had been doing her wash in a basin on the table. Among the clothes in the soapy water was the blouse Bergelon had so often seen her wear.

"Take a seat. Shove all that stuff onto the bed."

Both chairs were piled high with clothes.

"I thought Jean was supposed to be meeting you in Paris."

"I saw him yesterday!" he said.

He could not explain, even to himself, why he felt so moved. But so it was. He looked about him, his glance resting for a moment on the window sill, where Cosson's feet had rested while he read the newspaper article. How was it that the woman next door was not to be heard holding forth on the subject of her daughter's shortcomings?

"Do you mind if I go on with my wash while the water is still hot?"

She was watching him, no doubt wondering what he had come for but doing her best not to show it.

"What did he tell you?"

"That he was about to leave for Africa."

"I knew from the start that something of the sort was bound to happen, sooner or later. With his temperament, he couldn't have stayed on here."

She spoke quite dispassionately, with no hint of hatred, sadness, or rancor. She was merely stating a fact—though perhaps with just a touch of regret.

"I must point out that it would still have happened, whatever the circumstances. He was always restless, wherever he was. . . . He was always discontented. . . . He somehow needed to do everything to excess."

As she talked she rubbed the clothes between her hands. Now she paused in her work and looked at Bergelon. At this the doctor felt a sudden twinge of shame. It seemed to him that Cécile's glance implied:

"And you?"

It was as if he had betrayed Cosson, deserted him. He, after all, was here! He had returned home!

"Did you really believe he would kill you?"

"No!"

"You were wrong. He would have done it. He had it in him, just as he had it in him to kill me. Do you want matches? Over there, on that shelf on the left, in the vase."

As he went to get the matches from the vase, he wondered what it was in these commonplace words that filled him with a sudden sense of well-being. They were an indication that his presence was accepted, that there was nothing remarkable about it. It was a tacit acknowledgment that he was welcome to share the intimacy of her room.

He lit a cigarette and crossed over to look out the window, feeling perfectly at home.

"On Sundays, I always take advantage of my free time to do my wash," she explained.

The fact that she was dressed only in a transparent slip did not embarrass her in the least. After all, didn't she have to undress for Bergelon for her examination every Wednesday? She poured water into a saucepan, then lit the gas under it. The ice cream vendor's trumpet rang out at the end of the street.

"I doubt that he'll stay there long," murmured Bergelon, by no means certain that he believed what he was saying.

"I don't agree. I'm sure he will stay."

The bed was as she had left it when she had got up that morning. He thought for a moment. He hesitated. No, better not! There was plenty of time for that. . . . Besides, he had not really come to see her for that.

"Would you mind handing me those things on the chair? . . . I think I was the only one who really understood him. . . . Thanks. Where did I leave the soap?"

She found it, a cake of yellow soap hidden under the rim of the basin.

Several minutes went by. They chatted peaceably in the surrounding silence, their voices sounding like the purring of drowsy cats.

It was like waking from a dream when Bergelon, glancing at his watch, exclaimed:

"I'll have to be going!"

She did not say yes. She did not say no. It was all the same to her.

"If you have no objection, I would like to come here to see you from time to time. . . ."

She looked at him. Had she been expecting it? Or did it strike her as odd?

"You're always welcome—except in the afternoon."
As if he didn't know!

"And not before ten in the morning, because I'm a late riser. . . ."

Nevertheless, a time would come when he would intentionally visit her before ten, so as to surprise her, still damp from sleep, as she came to the front door to collect her bottle of milk and loaf of bread.

"Good-by, Cécile," he said, holding out his hand.

Since her hands were covered with soapsuds, the best she could do was to offer him her elbow.

"Good-by."

The time had not yet come for her to say anything more. She followed him with her eyes as he went out. Alone, bending over her bowl full of wash, she had plenty of time to think things over calmly and unhurriedly. Then she went to hang out her wash on the line stretched across the window, as she did every Sunday.

Bergelon felt very relaxed. For the first time in ages, he felt free in mind and body, and he strolled along looking in the shop windows, for he still had a good half hour to spare.

Looking back on his recent peregrinations, the idiotic risks he had taken—with Edna, for instance, a woman with no appeal for him, even as a partner in bed—then his adventures in Antwerp, he felt stunned at his own stupidity. What must Clarius, by now somewhere on the high seas, think of him? . . . To think that he had seriously considered going to Trebizond!

Trebizond! The very name was so absurdly farfetched.

The streets, all in shadow, were tinged with blue. For once, the pilgrimage to Herbemont had not ended in a downpour. The crowds were returning in a cloud of dust, their shoes powdered white with it.

Tomorrow . . . no, that was too soon. . . The day

after tomorrow he would pay a visit to Cécile. They would spend a pleasant hour or two together, like old friends. She was not the sort to treat him with familiarity in front of the other women and Superintendent Grosclaude during the weekly examination. He would, perhaps, exchange a smile and an almost imperceptible wink with her.

If he should ever be seen going into the house on Rue des Minimes, he could always pretend that he was visiting a patient. The one he would have to watch out for was his daughter. He suspected her of knowing a great deal more than anyone supposed, and, at the same time, of reading much more into things than actually existed.

Mechanically, he waved to someone in passing. But who was it, in fact, whom he had just greeted? He looked back and recognized the bulky rear view of Thioux.

Bergelon was wearing a hat. He had bought it in Paris, for he dared not return to Bugle, still less to his own house, without a hat. That was another thing that both Annie and Mile would find incomprehensible. Their father without a hat! At the same time he had bought himself a white shirt.

Many people were already home and had opened their shutters. Some must have noticed him walking up and down outside his house. No doubt they were asking themselves where he had been.

And where, in actual fact, *had* he been? He had been nowhere! He had made a wide semicircular detour around Bugle, solely for the purpose of going to Rue des Minimes from his own house. That was all.

Cosson, with his excitable temperament, had felt impelled to go to Africa! He had seen the same thing over and over again in his practice. Some patients conscientiously endured a lingering illness to the bitter end; others contented themselves with a short sharp fever, as a kind of inoculation.

Madame Pholien was also home, but it was scarcely worthwhile bothering her. He knew why Germaine and the children would be getting home a little later than the others. It was because they would be coming the long way around, so as to call in at Doutand, the pork butcher's, to buy ham. Germaine would have considered it demeaning to eat ham that came from anywhere but Doutand's. On Sundays, especially on the Sunday of the pilgrimage to Herbemont, they always had a light supper of cold ham and salad.

There was no need for him to go into the kitchen. He knew the soup would be ready on the gas ring, waiting to be heated up. The salad, thoroughly washed, would be in the wire basket, ready for Annie or Mile to shake it out in the yard, leaving a trail of water on the paving stones. One slice of ham per person, one a little thicker than the others. Germaine always made a point of this, because he was the man of the house and needed all his strength.

He saw them turning onto the street from the promenade beside the Loire. The red in the sky was beginning to deepen. He felt no more than a faint, irrational twinge of annoyance at seeing Monsieur Charles, who was very tall and was wearing a gray suit, walking in their midst, carrying the parcel of ham. Mile was hopping on one foot on the edge of the sidewalk, waiting for the inevitable admonition:

"You'll ruin your shoes!"

Annie looked limp and sullen, as she always did on Sunday evenings, for she hated walking.

He was undecided whether he should go to meet them or wait for them at the door. They had seen him. Mile broke into a run, then grabbed him by the hand.

"Hello! So you've come back. . . . Mother dreamed last night you would!"

Mile smelled of the countryside, of hay and crushed grass, faintly spiced with incense.

"Do you know how much edelweiss I sold? Guess!"

Mile had a passion for guessing games.

"Guess. . . . What do you think? Fifty? Jules Chantier sold fifty-two."

The others were catching up. He could distinguish their features more clearly now.

"I sold a hundred and five! And what's more, one old gentleman put a fifty-franc bill in my box. . . ."

Annie was holding Monsieur Charles's hand. She did not let go of it until she was within ten steps of her father; then she came forward, very dignified, to allow herself to be kissed. Was she, perhaps, a little disappointed? Maybe she found the substitute better company than her father.

For a moment, it looked almost as if Germaine was hiding behind Monsieur Charles.

"Good evening, Elie."

She put up one cheek, then the other, at the same time fumbling in her bag for her key.

"How do you do?" said Monsieur Charles, looking faintly embarrassed.

And that was all there was to it! Except for the additional presence of Monsieur Charles, it was a Sunday evening just like any other. There was the usual draft when the door was opened. And there was Germaine, no sooner across the threshold than making a dash for the kitchen to light the gas under the soup, before even taking off her hat.

Annie, whimpering as usual, could not wait to get her shoes off. Mile was blowing shrill blasts on his Scout whistle.

"Would you believe it, only last night I dreamed . . ."

"So Mile told me."

"You must admit it's an odd coincidence."

She lacked the courage to look him in the face. Perhaps she did not feel entirely in control of herself and feared that she might burst into tears.

"I must go up and change. I won't be long. Please excuse me, Monsieur Charles."

Monsieur Charles, disproportionately tall for the house, stood in the doorway flushed and awkward, his sparse, fair hair brushing against the transom.

"Have you heard," he asked, his Alsatian accent adding to the solemnity of his tone, "that Madame Portal died last night?"

So that was why the house was all shut up.

"Her husband didn't get home until two in the morning, and by that time it was all over."

Germaine, calling from upstairs:

"Annie! Hurry up and set the table, dear."

And Annie, grumbling:

"Why does it always have to be me? I don't see why, just because Mimile is a boy, he should never . . ."

Her eyes were red, but she was smiling. She must have had a little cry, all alone up there, afterward washing her eyelids. She had even taken the trouble to powder her nose. Still resolutely smiling, she kept looking at Bergelon, as if to say:

"You see? We're all so happy to have you back. It's grand."

The only slight awkwardness was the presence of Monsieur Charles, who had to be shown to his new place at the table, thus making it clear that during Bergelon's absence he had occupied the doctor's chair, opposite the window and the chicken run.

"Have you heard about poor Madame Portal?"

She was not yet wholly reassured. She claimed that she

was not hungry, to divert attention from the fact that, owing to her husband's return, they were one slice of ham short.

"The children and I got your cards. . . . I explained to them about your having to attend a congress in Antwerp, and told them that you had taken the opportunity to . . ."

She swallowed, fought back her tears, and managed to force another smile. And she glanced covertly at Monsieur Charles, as if to apologize, as if to thank him again for all his help, for there was no doubt that she had taken him into her confidence.

"Why haven't you brought us back any presents?" protested Mile, frowning.

"Your father had no time. . . ."

"Did you leave your luggage behind ın Riva-Bella?" asked Annie in surprise, suspecting something amiss.

"Yes, of course! Naturally!" exclaimed Germaine. "Why shouldn't he, since we're all going there next week?"

He had not thought of this. Their real vacation, as a family, was yet to come.

"I'm not sure I'll be able to spare the time. ."

Surely, she must know that Edna . . .

"Monsieur Charles has agreed to stay on for another month   His mother will be coming here to look after him. . . . You did get my letter, didn't you? You can't imagine what a splendid woman she is. . . ."

Could she sense his uneasiness?

"Oh, by the way, when I was in Riva-Bella, I did as you asked and got in touch with that patient of yours . . . Madame Edna Chevrières or Chennevières. . . ."

She flushed as she spoke the name.

"She was due to leave for the Riviera with her son at the end of last week."

Poor Germaine! She was not going to give up. She was

determined to settle the matter there and then, in front of everyone, in her own cryptic way, so that they would not have to revert to the subject when they were alone together. He knew that she would never again mention what was now past and done with, except, perhaps, during a quarrel, and then only by a sigh or an obscure hint.

"Mimile is hoping to get at least two first prizes, and a second. . . ."

"You promised, if I did, that I could have a bow and arrow," Mile pointed out.

"Of course! A little more salad, Monsieur Charles?"

She felt a little ashamed of herself for not having asked her husband first.

"What about you, Elie? I used walnut oil for the dressing."

"I noticed."

"Who's going to get the mousse from the cellar?"

This was also part of the ritual. On the Sunday of the pilgrimage, she always made a mousse the night before and put it in the cellar to chill.

"Me!"

"Me!"

The two children always fought over the mousse. They wrenched open the cellar door so violently that the whole house shook.

"You won't get more than your fair share anyway!" Annie could be heard to exclaim.

"Neither will you!"

"Let go of the dish!"

They could have used some light, but the lights had not yet been turned on. The three grownups were left in peace in the dining room for a few minutes. Monsieur Charles looked uncomfortable. He had a piece of gristle from the ham in his mouth, and he did not know how to get rid of it. In the end he swallowed it, visibly choking.

Germaine took advantage of the children's absence to smile at her husband. It was not exactly a smile, it was more an expression of contentment, relief, and gratitude, almost an unspoken prayer.

"Dear God, help us to . . ."

How many Hail Marys had she murmured under her breath as she climbed the steep pathway to Herbemont, stopping to kneel at all the stations of the cross?

His only worry was that, during the vacation, he would have no opportunity of going to Rue des Minimes. But he would delay his departure by four or five days. It would be overshooting the mark to invite Cécile to join him in Riva-Bella. And besides, there was the expense to consider.

He had been very careful to spend as little as possible. In fact, when Germaine saw how much he still had left in his wallet, she would be amazed. He had parted with less than three thousand francs! Twenty-three hundred, or twenty-four hundred at most—and that included his buying a shirt, a tie, and a hat, not to mention the pair of new shoes he was wearing! And then there was the suitcase he had left behind at the Oude Antwerp. . . .

"Turn on the light, Annie."

Annie did so, and the pink-shaded lamp filled the room with a warm glow. Mile put the bowl of mousse down on the table.

"Help yourself, Elie."

She turned to Monsieur Charles and said graciously:

"Help yourself, Monsieur Charles."

Where was Cosson now?

But why dwell on Cosson? He no longer seemed quite real. Cosson, with his gold deposits, the two thousand Negroes, mostly dressed in rags, the shanties, shacks, and mud huts, the phonograph blaring out Viennese waltzes, military marches, and operatic arias, the Portuguese trader behind the counter ...

He blushed. He had just remembered a name. In fact, he could hear it ringing in his ears, as though someone had actually spoken it aloud:

Trebizond.

And there was Germaine's voice, the voice she assumed when she wished to show herself especially affable, pursing her lips in a refined manner:

"Help yourself to some more, Monsieur Charles. I'm not having any. I hardly ever touch sweets."

Trebizond, indeed!

Nieul-sur-Mer, 1939